The soft fullness of her lower lip distracted him when he needed to be relentless.

He remembered the feel of her against him when he'd shuttled her behind the tapestry earlier. The scent of her beside him during dinner. The taste of her mead tonight reminded him of a long-ago kiss. He had walked away from her easily enough five years ago, certain he'd been wronged. As a man in his prime he had not worried over the loss of a woman who was little more than a girl at the time.

But seeing Cristiana now—her strength, her full-grown beauty—had put him in a strange distemper. Because no matter how sweetly innocent Cristiana appeared on the outside, she possessed the heart of a warrior.

* * *

In the Laird's Bed
Harlequin® Historical #1026—January 2011

Author's Note

As an author of medieval romance, I have frequently been inspired by the Arthurian legends. Last winter I reread *Sir Gawain and the Green Knight,* and really enjoyed the idea of a stranger who appears on a dark winter's night to issue a challenge. The set-up for *In the Laird's Bed* was the result of that inspiration.

From there, however, Cristiana and Duncan took full control of their story. Both have secrets to keep, a task that becomes dangerously difficult as heat flares between them. Life in this medieval keep quickly becomes a pressure cooker, with nowhere else to go for miles in the thick of a Scots winter.

I hope you enjoy *In the Laird's Bed,* and don't forget to learn more about my upcoming releases at www.joannerock.com.

Happy reading,

Joanne Rock

In the Laird's Bed

JOANNE ROCK

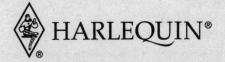

TORONTO • NEW YORK • LONDON
AMSTERDAM • PARIS • SYDNEY • HAMBURG
STOCKHOLM • ATHENS • TOKYO • MILAN • MADRID
PRAGUE • WARSAW • BUDAPEST • AUCKLAND

Recycling programs for this product may not exist in your area.

ISBN-13: 978-0-373-29626-2

IN THE LAIRD'S BED

Copyright © 2011 by Joanne Rock

**Did you know that some of these novels
are also available as ebooks?
Visit www.eHarlequin.com.**

For Ann Leslie Tuttle and the editorial team at
Harlequin Historical who make my work such a pleasure.
Thank you for sharing your wisdom
and your passion for stories!

Prologue

The scent of her beckoned.

Even from the desolate rocky outcropping beneath the guard tower of Domhnaill, Duncan the Brave caught Lady Cristiana's fragrance on the wind. The intoxicating smell was no herb-laden soap or rose-strewn bath, however. It was the scent of her fabled mead that rolled down the cliff side, surrounding Duncan and his men in a cloud of steamed clover and honey.

Who could have guessed a woman who brewed such heavenly delights would refuse a man shelter?

"Tell her I ask in the name of Christian charity," Duncan called to the surly guard who did not wish to admit them to the ancient seat of the Domhnaill family. The grizzled old keeper of the gate had left

Duncan's men waiting many long, cold minutes while he exchanged messages with his hard-hearted lady.

"'Tis the laird who does not wish to shelter his enemy," the guard returned, even as Duncan knew the man lied. Rumors of the old laird's poor health had traveled far. He did not rule his own keep anymore. "He bade me inform you there is a monastery nearby—"

"On the other side of a mountain," Duncan pointed out, giving his frustration vent. "Tell your laird and his heartless daughter that I will gladly hand over my armor for the chance to thaw the icicles from my cloak until the storm passes."

Curse the Domhnaill pride.

In the five years that had passed, they had not forgiven the wound suffered by their family when Duncan's brother had tested the bridal bed with Cristiana's sister before their nuptials. They'd declared the marriage contract void and took the lovers' act as a declaration of war, widening a long rift between their clans.

Wind whistled down the rocks, swirling in erratic bursts around his men's feet and lifting the horses' manes to blow wildly. Icy snow had fallen hard all day, making their march north impossible. Duncan had no choice but to seek shelter and wait out the storm.

Just as he'd planned.

Above them, the old guard disappeared and—after

a few more moments—a new face appeared through the frosty veil of snow. The figure leaned through the guard-tower window, prompting a long fall of cinnamon-colored hair and gold silk scarves over the casement. The heavy fur hood she wore over her head did little to contain the lush, unbound locks in the fierce weather.

The mistress of the mead herself.

Cristiana of Domhnaill did not greet him with a smile.

"You will submit every last blade and arrow, sir," she commanded in a tone that suggested she was not accustomed to being disobeyed. "And even then, you will find our hospitality is limited for oath-breakers."

"You look well, my lady." Duncan bowed in the saddle, a difficult task considering his bones had frozen stiff a few leagues back. "I've no doubt your hospitality will be as generous as your forgiving heart."

"I'm pleased we understand each other. I will lower the bridge, but you must await my men for the disarming before you set foot upon it." At her words, the bridge mechanism gave a mighty creak, the big gears moaning in protest. "We sup late to welcome the new year and you may join us then. I have guests within, sir, and would not have admitted you except that I cannot afford to appear uncharitable."

In a swirl of golden veils and cinnamon strands,

she departed, leaving the day colder still in her wake. She was not present to see Duncan's satisfied grin.

"Our gamble has rewarded us with success." He crossed himself in gratitude, since the risk could have been a lethal one. For although he'd hoped to plead a traveler's need for admittance to the Domhnaill stronghold, he had not anticipated how quickly the cold and snow would come upon them. The unforgiving Highland winters had laid more men low than enemy blades.

Beside him, one of his best knights snorted.

"You call it success that we've been lured into the lap of the enemy with naught to defend ourselves?" Ronan the Lothian eyed the armed guards riding over the lowered drawbridge with suspicion. "I've always known you were hell-bound, Duncan, but I thought you would at least go to your death with sword raised and curses flying."

"Some battles cannot be won with a blade." Unbuckling his sword belt, Duncan hoped he could trust his instincts on Cristiana's character.

He'd known her only briefly five years ago, but she'd once pledged herself to him with a sweetness he'd never forgotten. Had it not been for his brother's actions, both he and Duncan would have been wed to Domhnaill women for many moons by now.

Calamity would not have befallen his people. The men and riches of this keep would have protected his lands.

Ronan scowled as he withdrew an ice-encrusted dagger hilt from a strap at his thigh.

"Aye. And in this case, your enemy might be subdued with the only sword you'll still possess when we are finished here." Ronan lowered his voice as the Domhnaill guards drew closer to retrieve the growing pile of steel.

Divested of all his weapons, Duncan guided his horse up onto the bridge planks.

"'Twas such a tactic that created trouble last time." He'd never understood why the Domhnaills felt the need to break a betrothal contract for their daughter, when the union had only been consummated early.

Their excuse had been that Donegal was too rough in the taking. But what pampered virgin did not complain thus after her first time?

Nay, insufferable Domhnaill pride had cost them all dearly. Even Cristiana, whom Duncan had treated with naught but fairness, had cried off their betrothal. She'd somehow convinced her father that the Culcanon family had come to Domhnaill only to further the long rift between the families, and that Duncan would surely treat her unkindly one day if they were to be man and wife. The old laird—even then, well ruled by his daughters—had called off the alliance and refused the marriages. And that action had marked the beginning of all the problems that had torn apart Duncan's clan these past three years.

But not for much longer. With a secret token

concealed on a thong beneath his tunic, he possessed a key to solving the matter of his ravaged lands and divided people. A map that would lead him to the long-buried wealth of a generations-old ancestor whom he shared with Cristiana. All he needed was enough time to search it out before she banished him from her keep forever.

Chapter One

The steaming scent of cloves and ginger sprinkled on her latest brew brought Cristiana none of the usual pleasure. She breathed in the fragrant bouquet wafting over the boiling honey and water, testing for the right mix of heat and herbs to her most popular mead. But although the balance smelled fine now, she feared this batch would be bitter in the end. In her experience, the best meads were brewed when her heart was light and, right now, worry weighed her down more heavily than the ice-coated fur she'd worn outside into the storm.

The presence of an enemy under her roof had not been far from her mind this past hour as she'd hastened to oversee final preparations for an elaborate meal. She had to run the keep for her invalid father while maintaining the duties of a lady, since her mother had died many years ago and her sister had been sent far away after being ruined by Duncan the Brave's callous kin.

How dare he call upon her now after siding with his brutish half brother? Cristiana would be hard-pressed to hide her secret from Duncan while he took shelter here.

Stirring the bubbling mead mixture one last time, Cristiana left the squat brewery tower her father had built to encourage his daughter's gift. He had tried to dissuade her from mead-making for years, declaring the interest to be the purview of lesser men's daughters. But when the lords of the realm began requesting it for purchase and foreign kings sent gifts to obtain a small store, her sire had seen the wisdom of indulging her.

Now she raced through the keep to attend her guests, knowing she would not have time to change before the meal. It had been all she could do to hide the evidence of her secret from her new visitor and his men. The preparations had been hasty and not as thorough as she would have liked, but her temporary arrangements would hold at least until after they supped.

The New Year's feast had always been celebrated at Domhnaill with great festivity, and Cristiana could not afford any changes in routine that would hint at her family's struggles.

Wiping her brow of the perspiration accumulated

from her dash to the great hall, she straightened a tapestry and measured what else was left to do before the meal. Quickly, she handed off her fur cloak to a giggling server who pinched and teased a squire of one of the guests. Cristiana gave the maid a stern look that held the promise of more work if she did not mind herself.

"You were that young once, my lady."

The rich roll of a deep male voice came from behind her, startling her even as it called forth a wealth of memories that made her feel foolish. Oh, how she had craved that voice in her ear once upon a time.

Turning, she faced her enemy full-on without the safety of her guard tower and a moat separating them.

Duncan the Brave, the legitimate son of Malcolm Culcanon, rose from a seat he'd taken in the shadowed corridor outside the great hall. His shoulders blocked the light from the nearest torch, casting his tall, formidable frame into a dark outline. Five years had taken little toll on his handsome features. Women all over the Highlands vied for his attentions ever since he'd been a youth. Cristiana herself had found him most pleasing when they'd met. The keenness of his dark green gaze mirrored his fine intellect. His close-cropped brown hair lacked the flowing beauty of more vain men, but Cristiana appreciated the cleanliness apparent in the sheen of it. Most of all, she admired the warrior strength of him, his chest so solid, it felt as if he wore chain mail upon it or rather, it *had* once upon a time when she'd ventured a touch. She'd hardened her heart to this arrogant man and all his family long ago.

"Fortunately, I was never that foolish." She turned from him to welcome two other guests who'd been invited for the winter revelry, a neighboring lord and his lady, who had supplied Domhnaill with men and allegiance for generations.

"Duncan!" the velvet-swathed mistress, Lady Beatrice of the Firth, gushed with delight upon recognizing Cristiana's companion. She clamped a heavily jeweled hand to her breast as if to quiet her heart. "How good to see you. We have heard about your success in driving the Normans from our borders—"

"We must take our seats," her husband interrupted, his low tone laced with warning. "Duncan has only sought shelter because of the storm. No doubt, he is weary with travel."

Forestalling the argument that appeared imminent from Beatrice, Peter of the Firth dragged his wife into the hall.

"If you are stirred by the dance music, my lord," Beatrice called over her shoulder with a simpering smile, "I will be most glad to partner you."

Cristiana would have taken the exchange as an excuse to sidestep Duncan, but he must have sensed her motive, for he clamped a broad hand about her wrist and tugged her back into the shadows behind a giant tapestry.

"Sir," she protested, yanking her hand back and finding it well caught.

Alarm pricked over her skin. No one could see them here. Would he brutalize her as his half brother had brutalized her sister? He had made no secret of his fury over her choice to break their betrothal.

"We need to speak freely before we dine." He spoke into her ear, holding her much too close. "I am prepared to do you homage tonight as a peace offering. Will you accept?"

She tried to quiet her alarm by recalling how many important lords and ladies were on the other side of the tapestry. Duncan could not possibly mean her harm. Taking a deep breath, she calmed herself. And in the space of a heartbeat, she noticed the laundered scent of a fresh tunic and the warmth of his powerful form beneath it. His fingers spanned the inside of her arm while his thigh brushed against her skirts.

Her heart thundered at the audacity of his suggestion and his closeness.

"I will offer you shelter and nothing else." She tried not to think about the last time he'd held her thus. The sweetness of the kiss that had made her long to be a wedded woman back before she knew how faithless a Culcanon could be. For all that Duncan had expressed outrage at her refusal to wed, he'd wasted no time in reuniting with his lover at a nearby keep. "Do not take a charitable action for granted, lest you find your men escorted from my gates with all haste."

"It would not be wise to rebuff the king's new ally in front of so many witnesses, Cristiana." His hold on her eased. "Perhaps you have not received news of the kingdom since your father has been ill, but I assure you, Malcolm is unifying his holdings and carving a new order. The world has changed much in five years."

On the other side of the tapestry, more guests arrived and a minstrel struck up a bright tune sure to draw the rest of the keep to the hall for holiday revelry.

As early as this morning, a smoothly run supper to distract from her father's continued absence would have been her biggest concern. Now, Duncan suggested her efforts fooled no one, and worse, her family's standing might be suffering for the lack of a Domhnaill presence near King Malcolm.

"You forget yourself, sir." She slid free of his grip and busied her nervous hands by straightening her belt. "The Domhnaills have long been loyal supporters to the crown. And although we never troubled the king with the injury your kin did to mine, it is not too late for us to appeal for justice if you wish to bring the matter to his attention."

She had not forgotten the hurts her sister had suffered. The humiliation. The bruises. The recollection steeled her spine and deafened her ears to the other memories of that summer when the Domhnaill women had admitted treacherous men into their hearts.

"Cristiana, do not allow old angers to blind you. Domhnaill needs a leader, and if your da does not choose a successor, the king will find one for him."

The possibility so closely echoed her deepest fears that she felt Duncan had breached her walls for the second time today.

Indeed, she was so rattled that she did not protest when Duncan took her arm to lead her away from the tapestry and into the dim corridor once more.

"I am flattered to be your dining partner this eve," he announced loudly, as if they'd been in the middle of a conversation. By taking advantage of her tongue-tied state, he'd just claimed the seat beside her at sup.

Cristiana knew she needed to regain her wits before he commandeered the whole holiday revel.

The minstrel's song had reached a high note and the great hall was nearly full. Laverers circled the tables, offering a basin and towel to diners wishing to wash up.

"A poor traveler will always find a meal and a warm hearth at Domhnaill," she returned with forced brightness, holding herself stiffly away from him.

How did he know so much about the problems here? Swallowing back her fear, she allowed herself to be guided through the diners, toward the dais. Green pine garland hung from the rafters, infusing the room with the scent of a forest. A jongleur whom she'd named master of the revel was leading the servers in a song of welcome while guests found their seats.

"The hearth is all that is warm these days," Duncan whispered for her ears alone. "I remember when that was not always so."

She stiffened.

"You've no right—" she began, but cut herself off as a server approached them. The maid carried a heavy flagon of mead, reminding Cristiana of her first duty as hostess.

Duncan must have remembered, as well, for he leaned close again, not bothering to hide his nearness from her guests.

"Perhaps you will recall some of the old warmth when you must serve me?" He eased away from her, but masked his callousness with a low bow over her hand.

Fearing he might kiss her fingers in the courtier's way, she snatched her hand back at once. But Duncan only smiled and took his seat at the high table.

Cursing him roundly under her breath, she accepted the pitcher of mead and approached the dais. The lady of Domhnaill had always served her guest personally to begin meals in this ancient hall, and Cristiana had no intention of straying from the tradition when she had fought so long and hard to show the world everything ran smoothly here.

"To your health, my lord," she intoned, even managing to dip her head slightly in his direction as she did so. Thankfully, the forced curtsy helped to hide her burning cheeks.

With hands that hardly quivered, she approached Duncan the Brave and poured him a cup of her finest mead as if her world wasn't falling apart. As if her father wasn't dying. As if her beloved sister hadn't been exiled.

And almost as if Cristiana wasn't raising her sister's illegitimate babe in secret.

Chapter Two

The sweetness remained. Yet there was more to it than that.

Duncan rolled the honey mead on his tongue hours later, after the meal had ended and the dancing commenced, trying to identify what was different about Lady Cristiana's famed brew from the last time he'd had a taste. He watched the lady herself as she bowed serenely to her dancing partner, an elder of her clan who served as a close adviser to her father. Like her mead, Cristiana was more complex than he recalled. Time had erased the softness of girlhood from her face, leaving a more elegant and refined beauty. She moved with grace and ease as she danced, though her serious expression made him think she was more apt to be discussing war strategy than holiday celebrations.

Neither she nor her smooth libation were as simple as a sum of their parts. No single facet could be clearly defined. But the effect of the whole was intriguing. Potent. He could feel the sweet sting of the wine in the pleasing stir of his blood.

Then again, he might be confusing the effect of the woman with her beverage.

"You promised me a dance, my lord."

The husky feminine voice in his ear was not the one he wished to hear just then. Turning, he was abruptly placed at eye level with Lady Beatrice's considerable cleavage. She batted her lashes and extended her hand, forcing him to either dance or refuse her publicly.

Or…neither.

"Lady Beatrice." Replacing his empty cup upon the table, he rose to his feet. "I regret that I cannot, for I must act on a New Year's tradition right now. But I trust you will not be disappointed in the game." The custom of a New Year's game or challenge aided the second part of his plan.

"My dear sirs and gentlewomen." Duncan raised his voice over the dying strains of music from the last dance. Accustomed to ruling over a hall, he did not mind stepping into the laird's shoes. "I wish to thank your good lady for sharing the richness of her hospitality and the merry mood of her hall."

His words were echoed round the room, though not very heartily by Lady Beatrice, who appeared disgruntled about the lack of a dance. Over near the minstrels, Cristiana accepted the praise with a demure nod, but Duncan spied her discomfort over having him here.

But she did not deserve an easy heart after the way she had severed all ties to him on the basis of her sister's fickle moods.

"And in the spirit of the season," he continued, hiding bitterness beneath a hearty tone, "I ask your lady's indulgence of a boon."

Cristiana's head whipped up, instantly alert. Her gaze swept the hall, perhaps searching for aid among her father's men. But who would escort him off the dais now that she had invited him there? Half her guards were full of drink and the other half were wooing maids in darkened corners.

Duncan pressed on, determined to have his way.

"There has been a shadow between our families that I one day hope to lift. For now, I ask only that you grant me a moon and a day at Domhnaill to place a wondrous treasure at your feet." He quieted his voice in deference to the challenge, the storytelling skills of his Scots ancestors not missing him entirely. "If, at that time, my offering does not suit you, I will leave your keep forever. But if you are well pleased, I ask that our clans forge a new peace and heal the old rift once and for all."

As he finished his proposition, every eye in the hall turned to Cristiana. To her credit, she schooled her features admirably before attention swung her way. But Duncan had seen the flash of fury that had snapped in her gaze first.

He could not have called her out more neatly if he'd thrown a gauntlet at her feet. The public request for a boon at a holiday was something no chivalrous court could deny. Especially in front of such a large company of royal allies.

A bit of revenge felt good for an old slight.

"I am impressed by your earnestness," she replied, dropping a curtsy where she stood, her heavy golden skirts sweeping the floor.

Was he the only one who heard the sarcasm drip from her words like yeasty foam overflowing down the sides of a brew-filled cup?

Her elder adviser whispered in her ear as she straightened. Did the graybeard tell her to cast Duncan out into the storm? Or counsel public agreement until they plotted privately to oust him from their stronghold?

He might not ever know, since Cristiana shook her head and frowned at whatever the adviser suggested. Instead, she gestured to her guests.

"With all these souls as our witness, so it shall be." She waved to the minstrels and the trio raised their lutes. "Until then, I invite you all to dance."

It was the kind of general summons to merriment a hostess made on such occasions, but considering Lady Beatrice's coiled pose beside him and her readiness to pounce, Duncan took Cristiana's offer quite literally. Striding purposely toward her, he caught her before she could leave the dancers and spun her into the stately round.

Could he help a desire to gloat after all the grief she had caused his family? Cheated of the Domhnaill wealth a bride would have brought him, Donegal had turned on his own clan, robbing the Culcanon lands of all wealth while Duncan had been off at war these past three years. Duncan's efforts at war had been thwarted by his lack of men and arms, making his rise to prominence difficult and—worse—costing more men's lives in the long run.

"You are a knave of the lowest kind," she snapped softly at him when they passed close together on a turn. "What purpose can you possibly have to take up residence here?"

Duncan saw the heat in her glare. The resentment. Had she not taken enough vengeance already for the perceived insult to her sister?

Even, he recalled, passionate eagerness?

He had time to debate the answer as the dance did not place them near one another again for some moments. When she returned, eyes bright with emotion and cheeks flushed pink, she placed her hand upon his for a slow, methodical turn.

"Our clans were once bound together for a reason." He had not planned that response, but the words left unchecked. "This stretch of coast is treacherous and must be guarded by one strong force, not two divided clans. The rift between families should have ended with alliances."

She skipped a step, her expression one of unguarded surprise before emotions shifted and churned.

Seeing they were at the end of the line of dancers, Duncan stole her hand and hauled her away from the revelry. He didn't stop at the trestle tables or even the dais swathed in embroidered silks, but continued out of the great hall.

Just outside the hall, she halted.

"Nay. I am not some idle-minded maiden to follow where a strong knight leads, just because he wills it." She wrenched her fingers from his grip with more force than necessary.

"Lady, you are far too calculating and coldhearted a lass to be accused of an idle mind." Resentment made him incautious. But then, his family had never been known for their restraint. "If you would rather speak of this in full view of your household, let us do so."

He pivoted to face her. Arms crossed. Impassive. She did not speak.

"Perhaps we should take the discussion to your father?" he prodded, wondering how long she could hide the old man from him. "The laird is best suited to speak for his people anyhow."

He half wondered if the laird was even in residence. None of the people in her hall tonight had remarked upon his absence. Were they so accustomed to being ruled by an unwed maid and an old adviser that they did not think it strange?

She bristled. Straightened.

"Very well."

The soft fullness of her lower lip distracted him when he needed to be relentless. He remembered the feel of her against him when he'd shuttled her behind the tapestry earlier. The scent of her beside him during dinner. The taste of her mead tonight that reminded him of a long-ago kiss. He had walked away from her easily enough five years ago, certain he'd been wronged. As a man in his prime, he had not worried over the loss of a woman who was little more than a girl at the time. A girl he'd only planned to wed for political reasons. He'd had a lover at the time, anyhow—a widow, who had gladly eased the loss of Cristiana.

But seeing Cristiana now—her strength, her full-grown beauty—had put him in a strange distemper. She had robbed him of more than lands, gold and power. She had cheated him of sharing her bed.

"When?" he pressed, ready to seek her father's chamber now to call her bluff.

"I will ask the clerk for an appointment in the morning."

"Did you require an appointment with him earlier today when I arrived at your gate? Do marauders and warmongers need to see the clerk first, as well?"

"Since you are neither, it hardly matters." She

turned on her slippered foot as if to re-enter the hall. "And do not count on the chivalry of my court to protect you from any more outrageous proposals in the great hall. Underneath our fine manners, we are Scots the same as you. Our swords are just as swift."

With a snap of her skirts, she flounced away. And while he had accomplished his goal today of gaining access to Domhnaill and securing shelter long enough to search for a treasure, he had made a tactical error in underestimating his enemy. By dropping the guise of courtly visitor in need of shelter too soon, he had alerted her to more of his motive than he would have liked. Because no matter how sweetly innocent Cristiana appeared on the outside, she possessed the heart of a warrior.

"Father?" Cristiana tapped on the laird's tower door late that night. She knew seeing her da—healthy in body even if his mind was confused—would soothe the unease she felt from the day's disturbing events. He still had occasional moments of clarity that reminded her of the old days, when he was the most powerful laird on the eastern seashore and nothing could harm his family or his people.

"Netta?" he called to her from the other side. "Come in."

It was her mother's name. Her mother whom he beckoned. Still, Cristiana entered, crossing the planked floor covered in old tapestries to muffle the sounds of his ranting on his less lucid days. He was not a prisoner here, but for his own health he was well guarded. He'd escaped the keep to wander the coast once, and they'd thought him dead for sure.

"Father, it's Cristie." She righted a fallen flagon on a sideboard.

The chamber was dark as the fire had burned low. No torches were lit and she'd left hers outside. But as her eyes adjusted, she could see him seated at the slit in the wall where the tapestry had been pulled back to drape over the arm of his chair.

"A stranger walks the cliffs." Her father turned toward her, his snowy white hair in tufted disarray. Yet his eyes appeared focused, his voice clear. "Is it one of your guests? You should have guards at the walls, girl. I cannot watch over the grounds all night."

Dodging an open chest of weapons near the bed, Cristiana joined him at the window and peered out. Little land surrounded the keep at the southeastern side. A narrow strip of rocky ground ringed the tower before the land fell off sharply toward the sea.

Even from this height and under the light of a half-hearted moon, Cristiana recognized the broad shoulders of a man rumored to have fought at the English king's side as a favor to Scots sovereign.

"It is Duncan the Brave. He has returned from Edward's court to reap the benefit of his new standing with King Malcolm." She didn't know whether or not her father would understand the significance of her words, but he appeared more lucid than usual. And she did so sorely miss her strong, decisive father. "He is our guest for the next moon and has turned in his weapons. But I assure you, the walls are well armed, so you do not have to sit watch."

"That is your young man," her father observed, clearly remembering another time and confusing it with the present. "You see what a strong man I've chosen for you? You see how he would rather keep watch over you at night than sleep? A good man, that."

Disappointment burned the back of her throat as she realized she would find little to comfort her here tonight, aside from her da's good health. It had been this way for many moons with him—he would forget old friends and servants. He mixed up the past and present, occasionally demanding to know where Edwina was and why she hadn't been to see him. Forgetting that he himself had arranged for her exile after she'd given birth to Donegal of Culcanon's unclaimed babe.

"You have always tried to do what's best for me," she agreed, laying her head upon her father's shoulder as she watched Duncan prowl around the grounds in the darkness. "I have never denied it."

"But you did not come here to listen to an old man ramble." He gave her shoulder a squeeze and dropped a kiss on the top of her head. "What can I do for you, daughter?"

"Our new guest is most anxious to meet with you." She did not know how to put him off without stirring undue interest in her father's absences. "I wondered if he could stop by your chamber sometime when Connor is with you and you can explain to him about—er—that you're not feeling so well?"

Her father's adviser would do most of the talking and guide the conversation. But Duncan would at least see the laird with his own eyes and know the old Scots lord was not on his deathbed.

She would have one less secret to hide.

"Aye. Well enough. Send the lad around anytime. We need a strong leader here. Your old man can't protect the walls forever." He patted her shoulder absently and rose.

Cristiana remembered the time when her father had called for Duncan's head on a platter alongside his faithless half brother's. He had been livid to learn his daughter had been touched against her will, and he would have mounted an army to decimate the whole clan had it not been for his wife's sudden illness and a deathbed plea to let Edwina choose what form his vengeance should take. She had been the one who'd suffered, after all. And Edwina had chosen to have the matter handled quietly, using her bride price to pay for a place for her in the English court, where no one knew of her past.

Later, when Edwina had learned she was pregnant, their mother had already died and their father was so heart-stricken with grief he had hardly noticed Edwina's retreat to her rooms for two moons' time. It was in those weeks his daughters had made arrangements of their own to protect the child and ensure the eldest could escape the memories Domhnaill would always hold for her. If the laird suspected the truth, he'd said nothing, emerging from his mourning a changed man.

"I will send him later this week, Da," Cristiana assured him, her gaze still fixed on Duncan as her enemy stared up at the keep and then back out at the water. "And you don't have to protect the clan forever. You can name your successor now, and then you won't have to concern yourself with such worries anymore."

"And rob my daughter of her rightful place? 'Tis bloody well bad enough that Edwina has lost her Domhnaill home. I will not leave you with nothing after all I've done to make this fortress the strongest in the east. Your man shall be laird, girl. And every man who has ever served under me knows that is my wish."

She nodded mutely, touched by his declaration even as she recognized it for the confused rambling that it was. Her visits here were frustrating, but she never left feeling unloved.

"Thank you, Da." She hugged her father hard, grateful for every day she still had him.

"Go rest your head, lassie. You've had a long day."

Nodding, she stoked the fire in the grate before slipping from the room. She would make sure Keane was beside her sire when Duncan met him so that the laird did not have to do more than greet him. She could not have her father give his confused blessing on a marriage that could never take place.

No matter how strong a guardian Duncan might be for Domhnaill, Cristiana did not trust him. He'd come back to this keep for secret reasons he had not shared. She knew it in her veins.

Nay, she would not trust Duncan. Not with her heart, not with her father's legacy and most certainly not with the little girl who deserved the warmth of a family's love. What might Duncan and his brother do if they learned Cristiana had been harboring their heir for more than four years? Would they declare war on Domhnaill to get her back?

Or worse, was there a chance they spread their seed so carelessly that one more child bearing their distinctive green eyes would not matter to them at all?

For her niece, Leah's, sake, Cristiana refused to find out.

* * *

Duncan would turn this keep inside out to find what he sought.

He arose before the dawn the next morning, determined to make his time at Domhnaill as brief as possible. By the time he broke his fast and dressed warmly to fend off the frigid damp blowing in off the water, the sun's first rays lit the token he wore about his neck. He held up the medallion to the study the map worked in metal. The cryptic figure he believed matched some landmark on Domhnaill property.

A chill lingered on the breeze that had naught to do with the sea as he stalked farther from the stark gray walls. Unease lurked behind the keep's strong facade, a sense among the people that their leader had grown weak. Cristiana could make merry all the new year to hide her clan's shortcomings. But it did not change the fact that Domhnaill was ripe for the taking.

Duncan's eyes roamed over the stones of the keep in search of a pattern in the rock that might match the figure on his medallion. It was one of many possibilities for what the map might signify. And the task of studying stone walls did not require nearly enough of his attention to keep him from thinking about Cristiana.

About how she'd been ready to wed five years ago.

By the rood, he would never forget the heat of the

kiss they'd shared even though she'd been naught but an innocent maid. They'd been left alone to walk in the gardens, their families preoccupied with details of Edwina's marriage contract. Cristiana had not hesitated to take his arm when he led her through the fruit trees to a bench by an old wishing well.

Oddly, she had not recalled that it had been *her* to lead *him* there, since it had been that same day that Donegal had dishonored Edwina. Cristiana had accused Duncan of kissing her to distract her from keeping an eye on her sister. But it had not been so. Cristiana had been eager to be with him, her eyes bright with excitement as she drew him into the trees.

Not seeing any pattern in the stones now, Duncan found his feet picking out the path to that well. He needed to cover a lot of ground in the next moon if he hoped to find the treasure, so it made sense if he spent some of today taking in the lay of the land.

Breaking through the thicket of overgrown fruit trees, he spied a new building between the orchard and the well. A squat, round tower, the structure was too far from the keep to be a kitchen. Yet the smoke of a stoked fire puffed from a hole in the roof.

What construction had the old laird undertaken? Surprised at this sign of ambitious growth, Duncan made sure his medallion was hidden beneath his garments and approached the building, boots kicking up freshly fallen snow.

He tried the door, expecting it to be locked. Instead, the barrier swung open easily and the scent of sweet mead rolled toward him in fragrant waves. The scent of Cristiana.

Indeed, this was her domain. And she must have risen with the dawn like him to be at her work so early. But there she stood, all alone and toiling over a table, her shoulders bent to some work he could not yet see. She had not heard him enter, her full attention devoted to whatever project she labored over.

The building was a brew house unlike anything he'd ever seen before. It functioned as far more than a mere corner of a kitchen where special cauldrons were set aside for mead-making. The entire, fine structure appeared dedicated to Cristiana's brewing gift.

A hot fire burned in the center of the room, the blaze surrounded by protective stones to contain it. Some of the exterior wall of the tower was stacked with wood, but most of the walls were lined with other cauldrons.

The tower's only low windows were placed above a worktable near where Cristiana stood. The skin-covered openings allowed the dawn's light to spill over clay pots of dried herbs and spices. He could see now that she'd cut some sticks of cinnamon into smaller pieces, her hands dusted in fragrant powder.

"Cristiana." He spoke softly so as not to startle her, but her name became an intimate sound on his lips.

Startled anyway, she whirled around as if expecting to see a field full of marauding Danes.

"Duncan." Clutching a hand to her chest, she seemed to quiet her heart by force. "I am usually alone out here at this hour."

Her cheeks were flushed from the heat of the fire as she turned back to her worktable. An amethyst-colored kirtle swung about her feet as she moved, the fabric falling in time with her rhythmic cutting.

"You tend your potions well, Cristiana." He stepped deeper into the chamber, taking in the rainbow span of flowers drying on the rafters.

The scent of spices and dried berries mingled with the tang of yeast. Being in the brew house was like stepping into a late summer day with the rich warmth of the harvest all around.

"The Domhnaill mead is prized in trade. But I must use care in the making, since I can only obtain a certain amount of honey. Once I run out, I cannot replenish my stores until spring, so I dare not burn any."

Carefully, she scraped the worktable clean of the cinnamon she'd cut, swiping the last of the powder into her hand. When she'd gathered all she could, she brought it to a pot on the far wall and scattered it over the surface of the brew.

No wonder she carried such an enticing smell on her person at all times. She must absorb the fragrance right through her skin.

"Your father has invested a great deal in this trade." Peering up at the ceiling, he noted the excess rafters for additional space to dry herbs out of the way of the boiling cauldrons. Mortars and pestles, cups and small jars lined the shelves of an open cupboard.

"Our mead sells for a very good price. In turn, full coffers keep the men paid and attract strong alliances." She rinsed her hands in a bowl of water kept on the hearthstones and dried them on a linen rag tied to her girdle.

"Your father has not raised a fighting force in many years," he observed, pacing the perimeter of the structure to view the contents of the fermenting cauldrons. "His coffers must overflow with the excess. He could have made you a fine marriage long ago."

The dowry Duncan was to have received for her five years ago had been more than generous, especially considering his sons would have ruled Domhnaill one day. What would the laird offer to the man who wed Cristiana now?

"I do not think finding a husband for me is part of his purpose." Holding back her plaited hair in one hand, she bent over the cauldron in the center of the chamber and sniffed delicately.

The fabric of her tunic dipped away from her breasts as she leaned forward, presenting him with a view so beguiling he stopped cold in his pacing. A jolt of undeniable interest sparked. To lust after her was foolishness. She was no experienced woman to choose a man for pleasure's sake. She was an unwed maid, who must make a good marriage. A highborn one at that.

And he would suffer the fires of hell before it would be him after the cold way she'd dismissed him.

But the knowledge did not stop the heat streaking through his veins at the sight of her tempting, creamy flesh. The moment ended too soon as, straightening, she took up a spoon and stirred the concoction. He struggled to recall what they'd been discussing.

Ah, yes. A husband.

"Only a fool of a sire would ignore the need to see you wed. And your da is no fool." A stubborn, hard man perhaps. But other than the misstep with the broken betrothal, the old laird was a keen ruler. Or at least, he had been.

Perhaps she had sensed his gaze on her because she paused in her stirring to peer up at him. Though they stood many steps distant, he could feel the moment the air between them grew charged. As a virgin untouched, would Cristiana even know the source of such heat?

"I *choose* not to marry." Her words were so at odds with everything he'd been thinking, it took him a long moment to understand what she'd said.

"Impossible." He drew closer, telling himself he wished to judge her features and seek out the lie. Yet he knew he was pulled toward her by a power beyond his control. She fascinated him despite their mutual mistrust. "Your father has no sons. He has no choice but to ally himself—his people—with a strong clan who can protect the legacy of his lands."

She removed the spoon from the spinning, bubbling brew beside her and hung the instrument from a hook near the pot's handle.

"He will choose his successor when the time is right. I do not need to wed to secure our fate."

She spoke madness. Her father indulged this? He would question the old man about it when he obtained an audience with him, since it would make Duncan's work here easier if he did not have to fight off a suitor for control of Domhnaill. For now, he would have answers of a different sort from her.

She stared up at him with that steady, gray gaze of hers. She had become a practical woman. Efficient. Hardworking. But he remembered another facet of her. A passionate, unrestrained side that she'd locked down like it never existed after that day by the wishing well.

Suddenly, he had to know if that part of her still existed or if it had been stamped out forever by cool practicality.

"You would deny yourself a man's touch for all your days?" He reached toward her, telling himself he did so only to tease her. To make her feel a fraction of the frustration he'd felt years ago.

Her eyes remained locked on his. Perhaps she did not notice the approach of his fingers until he brushed a lock of her hair just above her temple. The touch had the sense of fate about it, and he recalled another touch, another kiss, another moment so similar to this one. The fact that Cristiana was no longer his did not alter a compelling urge to take her. To steal as much from her and the moment as she would allow.

Chapter Three

Cristiana held her breath at the feel of Duncan's fingers skimming her temple to sift lightly through her hair. To allow such a touch was foolishness, when they were utterly alone here. Her sister had been wooed to ruination once, and paid for it still. Would Cristiana follow in her footsteps?

Yet a part of her wanted to know if she had imagined the delight she'd once found in Duncan's caress.

Heaven help her, she had not.

"I understand there will be sacrifices with my choice," she answered finally, willing herself to step back, out of his reach.

But with her heart thudding a slow, insistent rhythm in her chest, she could not hasten her feet to do her bidding. There had been a time when she dreamed nightly of belonging to this man—body and soul.

"Do you?" He smoothed his thumb along her cheek and down to her jaw, stopping just below her chin. "Can you truly appreciate what you will miss when you've never experienced it?"

Heat sparked over her skin as he drew closer. From this distance, she could see the flecks of gold in his green eyes. Then her gaze flicked down to his mouth as she remembered the feel of his lips upon hers. His kiss had been exquisitely sweet. Patient. Stirring.

A new, small scar speared his top lip with a tiny white line. She found herself wondering what that marred skin would feel like against her mouth if he were to kiss her again.

Her heavy heartbeat sped faster, anticipation humming in her veins even as she reminded herself that he could play this game far better than she could. Five years ago hadn't he made her believe he cared about her, then raced away to another woman's arms without ever acknowledging Edwina had a legitimate complaint against Donegal's brutish behavior?

"I suppose it is easier not to miss something you've never had." Her voice was naught but a whisper between them, a quiet confession for his ears only.

Time dragged out. She wished for some kind of intercession to break the spell he'd cast over her. But perhaps if she indulged this once—if she made a decision to take some small pleasure from him on her own terms—she would not be so plagued with wonder about the attraction she couldn't deny.

"No good strategist makes a decision without adequate information." His gaze tracked hers. He handled her gently despite her fears about the Culcanon brutishness. "Perhaps you've forgotten the power of even one simple kiss."

His lips covered hers before she could argue the point. And wasn't it wicked of her that she did not want to argue it? The arrogant young laird could be mounting a takeover of her keep and yet all that concerned her right now was to test her fanciful memories of him against the truth of the flesh-and-blood man.

Pleasure flooded her faster than strong mead warmed the blood. At the feel of his mouth on hers, her knees wavered. His hand curved about her neck, holding her still for the quick, silken lash of his tongue along the fullness of her lip. She seemed to melt on contact, her whole body swaying until it found the steadying strength of his. Her lips parted, opening to his kiss.

In for a penny, in for a pound. At least this once.

Her fingers clutched at his cloak, seeking anything to steady herself. She gripped the fine wool in clenched fists as her body trembled beneath layers of the worn linen gown meant for working in the brew house. Now, that soft, much-washed fabric afforded her little protection from the raw masculine appeal of his muscular form. Her breasts pressed tight to his chest, the pleasant friction making her head spin with carnal thoughts no maid had a right to consider.

But the feel of her body against his consumed her. This was why she had not wanted to wed. The memory of her last kiss with Duncan had been thus and she feared it would not be the same with any other. For all that she was a maid, she knew deep down this kind of passionate potential did not exist between every man and woman. And—after once having the smallest taste of this soul-stealing excitement—she could not imagine settling for a cold coupling with some man twice her age.

"Cristiana." Duncan spoke her name over her lips between kisses. "You were meant to be touched. Kissed. Tasted."

Arching up on her toes, she brushed her mouth to his again, luring him back to wreak the skillful magic that made her senseless with desire. She just needed another moment. A last few stolen minutes to feel passion she'd never know again.

His hands locked about her waist. Holding her against him, yet restraining her from further contact. She blinked, confused.

"Why did you refuse me?" His voice was harsh, all traces of the silken-tongued suitor gone. "Why punish us both for a sin we did not commit? Was it not enough that Edwina broke her oath to Donegal? You had to break yours to me, as well?"

Her senses returned so quickly she felt a chill at the loss of passionate heat. She tried to wrench free, regret stinging sharp. His grip did not budge, however. Emerald eyes pierced hers, demanding answers she had already given.

"Do not pretend to have felt punished when you ran to your leman with the haste of a man who has been at sea for years," she accused. His defection to another woman's arms had rubbed salt in a wound since he had murmured sweet words in her ear the day prior about making love to *her*.

"You are so coldhearted that you would deny a man all comfort? Perhaps I should have sailed straight into battle afterward to take out my fury on an unsuspecting enemy?" His features were hard. Unforgiving. And bore no trace of the man she'd kissed.

Which was just as well. She would rather not face that man again anytime soon.

"The point is that you never gave up your lover when you were pretending to court me. And it was not *my sister* who broke the oath of the betrothal," she insisted. "'Twas Donegal who simply took what he wanted without respect to the marriage contract. For my part, I would never wed a man who would take his family's side so quickly he does not see the truth."

"I might say the same of you. Why are you so sure your sister did not find Donegal's bed willingly, only to regret it later? You have seen how persuasive a man's touch can be."

The sharp bite of his comment sank long teeth in an old wound. Anger erupted, giving her the strength to yank away.

"How flattering to know you only kiss with a purpose. But I will not defend myself or my sister to you again. You chose long ago to side with your brother who, I've since heard, has shown his true nature in your absence by bankrupting your lands and dividing your people. Yet you still believe he acted nobly in his treatment of my sister?" She stalked to the other side of the cook fire beneath the cauldron, needing a barrier between her and any man who could make her so angry.

She had lost so much, thanks to his need to humiliate her. Her family. And could he be so blind to Donegal's character still? How could she trust him with her own people if he couldn't discern clearly?

"He may have been a poor manager of people and lands. At the time, I could not see how that made him the beast your sister portrayed him as." He stalked to the cupboard and retrieved a vessel, then plunged it into an open pot of fermenting mead. "Besides, I saw Edwina depart the hall with Donegal myself that night they consummated their relationship. They stole kisses in the courtyard as they left. And I assure you, Edwina did not give those kisses begrudgingly."

"Stop." Cristiana refused to think on that night

anymore. She certainly did not want to consider the reckless, headstrong heart her sister had left with, only to return home with bruises and a soreness in her spirit that had never fully recovered. Her anger at Donegal had left Edwina unable to bond with his child, robbing her of the joy she should have felt in motherhood.

Edwina had begged Cristiana to raise her child. The choice had broken her sister's heart, but at least the decision had been a selfless one. Edwina had recognized that her exile from home and her broken spirit would not help her nurture the child. She had wanted Leah to have every advantage—a secure home, safety from her brutish father and a mother whose heart had not been frozen by violence.

So in order to protect the babe from its father and to salvage Edwina's reputation, Cristiana had vowed not to reveal Leah's existence until she was a woman grown. Indeed, the secret was not even hers to tell.

"Stop what? Forcing you to see that an innocent maid may not have understood where teasing kisses lead?" He threw back the contents of the cup and then slammed the empty container on the worktable. "You tossed away your future with both hands because of an incident that was as much Edwina's fault as anyone else's."

"Out." She could not muster more words than this. Not until she took a few steadying breaths and braced herself against a tall column supporting the rafters.

"You need to leave and never speak of it again if you wish to remain under my roof. Good day, sir."

"But it's not your roof, and never will be if you do not wed a strong man to rule Domhnaill for you. Perhaps I will put my own name forward as your father's successor to secure my shelter for the winter." He stalked from the brew house, turning briefly at the door. "I trust you've found a time for me to meet with him?"

"Tomorrow." She had hoped it would not be so soon, but perhaps a cold reception would send Duncan and his men on their way all the faster. "After we sup."

With a clipped nod, he pushed open the door, allowing a gust of bracing cold air to rush inside.

"And no need to worry about your place here, Cristiana. When I become laird here, I'm sure I'll still require a mistress of the mead. Or perhaps you wish to become my leman?"

The barb found its mark when she did not think he could hurt her any more.

"A wise man avoids making enemies with a woman who knows her herbs," she warned, cursing herself for ever opening her gate to him, let alone her arms. But he was already disappearing into the white swirl of a fresh snowfall outside her door.

Of all the cursed arrogance. How dare he threaten to depose her? Yet she'd committed the gravest mistake of the day. What had she been thinking to allow him to kiss and touch her, knowing he was a man of dangerously seductive skill? Of course, that had been much of the allure. The past had been hounding her ever since Duncan had arrived. Memories of their stolen moments together five years ago. The kiss that had taken place in this very spot.

Duncan thought she sacrificed much to remain unwed. In truth, after experiencing his kiss the first time, it had not been difficult to turn away other suitors. It had only been a hardship to know she would never wed *him*.

But he'd become her enemy that day her sister had returned home. She'd sworn then that no Culcanon would ever lay hands on the Domhnaill legacy. And no heated encounters with her former betrothed would sway her to forsake that vow.

At sup that eve, Cristiana would have been content to make excuses not to join her guests, except that the holidays were upon them and she had invited many of her father's allies to Domhnaill in the hope one of them would prove a strong successor for her father. She certainly had no desire to see Duncan again so soon after their earlier encounter.

But she had plotted many moons for this festive season with her father's oldest counselor, Keane, whom she waited for just outside the great hall. Unlike her sire, Keane had not lost his wits, his mind sharp as ever even if his sword arm lacked the strength to take over the keep himself.

The counselor appeared now, striding through the corridor with his irregular gait from an old battle wound. His white hair stood on end, shorn close to his head. He carried a knife at his hip even though it had been many years since he'd ridden off to war. He knew more about what had happened at Domhnaill five years ago than most, but he did not know about Edwina's child. Except for a midwife and her servant who had witnessed the birth, everyone else privy to little Leah's presence believed the girl an orphaned noble child left at Cristiana's door. A resemblance among clans and villages was not unusual, with many a laird spreading bastard children among his lands.

"Good eve, sir." She hastened to greet the advisor, drawing him aside and quickly explaining the meeting she'd arranged between Duncan and her father. "So if you could just remind the laird of his hatred of the Culcanons right before the meeting, I believe it will help our cause to send Duncan and his men packing."

The gnarled old knight folded his arms and cupped his jaw. Then shook his head furiously.

"Nay. 'Tis the last thing we want." He peered toward the great hall to ensure their privacy, then leaned closer to speak. "I know you girls broke off your marriage contracts after a quarrel with the young men, but do you think it wise to savor your spite for so long when Duncan is the most celebrated knight in the kingdom? What Domhnaill needs is a man like Duncan as laird."

For a moment, Cristiana wondered if Keane had succumbed to whatever wasting sickness her father had, for his words made no sense. But the shrewdness was still there in his lively blue eyes.

"Never." She did not need to explain herself. Still, something like cold fear gelled in her veins. "It is a family matter of the utmost delicacy, sir, but I cannot allow that."

More guests were arriving to sup as the vigorous chatter of some of the villagers mingled with the more refined cadence of the noble families' conversations. The scent of roast fowl and fish permeated the stone halls and beckoned revelers from all round.

"I may be an old man, missy, but I assure you, I can take a guess at what kinds of delicate matters go on that would offend a lady. I never thought it was right to break a contract the first time, but your father always had a soft heart for you girls. Now, I'm not saying you should marry the man. I'm just saying he would be the best possible choice for a successor."

When she started to argue, he backed up a step, that uneven gait of his biting her conscience as he hobbled backward.

"No sense getting up in arms," he protested, tugging on his tunic and smoothing it. "Just think about what's best for Domhnaill. Your da always did."

"Keane—" But she would have had to chase him to keep talking. The counselor hastened toward the hall.

"Look around at our other options this eve," he called over his shoulder as he kept on stumping along. "You'll see I'm right."

Frustration twisted her insides. They were nowhere near done with this conversation. True, she had not discovered a strong prospect to lead Domhnaill among her guests. That did not mean she would settle for arrogant Duncan, who'd maneuvered his way into staying here with the cunning of a serpent. Just because a man had the sword prowess of a champion did not mean he deserved any part of her homeland.

"Do you appear this angry at every feast in your hall, Lady Cristiana?"

The unwelcome question came from just above her left shoulder, where Duncan suddenly stood. He had appeared from nowhere as she wove through the crowd toward her seat on the dais.

The man moved with the stealth of a hunter.

"Only when I must host arrogant, demanding men over the holidays," she assured him, wishing his presence did not make her warm all over. She hoped her cheeks did not flush noticeably.

She would have hastened her step if there were not so many people nearby to see her indulge her temper. Hurrying away from her guests would hardly be considered good manners.

Instead, she forced a smile to her lips as Duncan looped her arm through his and escorted her to the dais table. She took the center seat when her father did not dine in the hall, which was most days now. Normally, she sat at her father's left and Keane to his right, but during the holidays, the dais table was full of high ranking guests. All of those seated had traveled with their wives for the promised festivities of the season, making the number of guests even and leaving the seat beside Cristiana vacant once again. Keane would have normally accepted an invitation to dine with her as her father's advisor, but he already sat with the knights. She had no choice but to pass another meal with Duncan.

"You think I demand too much?" He bent forward to grasp a handful of her skirts and lifted them slightly for her to slip one foot over the bench to take her seat. "You are free to make your own demands of me. In fact, I would welcome it."

The unexpected slide of her skirts up her ankle— by his hand, no less—caught her utterly off guard. Whatever strange battle he waged against her, she was clearly the less experienced tactician.

Settling into her seat as quickly as possible, she tugged back her gown in a small skirmish for the velvet under the table. In the end, he relinquished the cloth, but not before his knuckle grazed her thigh in a contact she felt all too well through the layers of linen and velvet.

"Is that so? Then prepare yourself, sir."

Before she could change her mind, Cristiana stood. She was the mistress of the hall in her father's absence. She could address the folk of Domhnaill if it served her. The noisy chamber quieted instantly as heads turned her way.

"My good people," she began, speaking to the high-ranking villagers mixed in the crowd as much as the lofty landowners from neighboring holdings. "I welcome Duncan of Culcanon again this night and have had more time to consider his request."

Beside her, he stiffened. Good.

"You have generously offered me a portion of the some mysterious treasure at the end of your time with us." There were a few gasps of surprise and a few cynical laughs. "But in the spirit of the holiday, good sir, we ask that you share some hint of what you seek before then? Your hunt can be our entertainment."

She sought answers and hoped this would be a way to obtain them. At very least, she had made her court aware of his intentions. No doubt he would not be able to search in secret if everyone in attendance knew what he was about. Perhaps his work would be so hampered by interested attendees that he would leave, frustrated and empty-handed.

For a moment—judging by the dark expression in his gaze—she thought she had succeeded in outfoxing him. But as he rose to his feet, his visage cleared and the carefree courtier appeared again.

Ready to take up her challenge.

"Good mistress, I would not deny you." Though he spoke to the assembled company, he stood close to her. Very close. As if they were lord and lady of this hall.

With an effort, she smiled up at him and wished she could tug herself away from him as strenuously as she had yanked her skirts from his fingers.

"Then how does your treasure hunting proceed? Tell us what you seek."

She had put him under the whole court's scrutiny. All eyes turned to him. Yet his gaze remained steadfastly upon her.

"For now, I can only tell these good people what I've found. Nay," he said, breaking his gaze at her to grin at the assembled folk. "Each day, I will show them instead."

Murmured interest rolled through the crowd as Duncan turned to her once more.

"Today, my friends, this is what I found."

Like a bird of prey, he swooped toward her so quickly she could do naught but panic. Wrapping her in his arms in front of the entire company, Duncan of Culcanon drew her to him and kissed her full upon the mouth.

Chapter Four

It was a small victory and it wouldn't last. But Duncan would never forget the sweetness in that moment he kissed Cristiana.

She'd been so surprised, her lips had parted in exclamation just before his mouth claimed hers. What man would not take advantage of such irresistible temptation? After what had transpired between them in the brew house earlier, he'd counted on the way her body stilled at his touch. He'd known she would not withdraw. Whatever awareness had sparked between them years ago became a potent force now.

When cheers and laughs erupted in the hall, he recognized it was time to retreat. With regret, he relinquished his hold on her.

Suspecting she would be angry all too soon, he savored a fleeting moment when her expression remained starry-eyed. For a moment, he could almost forget he attended her on a mission of deceit. That he'd come to wrest away her keep. Stuffing down those thoughts, he picked up his drinking horn to toast the company and deflect attention away from Cristiana.

"I am sure no other treasure I find will be half so rewarding." He raised his cup to a hearty round of cheers from his knights. "To the health of your laird and his lovely daughter."

Cristiana's face remained bright pink, but she drank to her father's health and motioned for the servers to start the meal. Upon taking his seat, Duncan noticed her hands shook slightly as she reached for the eating knife on the chain at her waist.

Not for a moment did he believe she trembled out of passion for him. Nay, he felt the anger emanating from her as surely as heat from the sun.

"You left me no choice." He dipped his head to explain, needing to remain in her good graces for at least a little longer. He had tested her patience in the brew house earlier, but just now he may have worn out what scant welcome he'd had completely. Though he'd arrived at Domhnaill with a large retinue of men, they were unarmed and therefore easier to uproot from a stronghold where they were not wanted.

And it was imperative he remain under her roof. He did not have the forces to take the keep from without.

All around them, diners exclaimed over yet another lavish feast for the holidays. The mighty Yule log still burned brightly in the hearth, echoing the flickering of torches ringing the great chamber. The scent of fragrant pine and honeyed mead mingled with the gingered spices of rich sauces and savory tang of roasted meats.

"You could have simply shared your task with the assembled guests when I asked. Or made up some fanciful lie to distract us from the truth." She did not look at him as she refilled his mead from a flagon left on the dais table. A fat silver ring set with rubies clanked against the hammered metal pitcher.

"I could not risk having the whole keep learn how deadly serious I am about my quest, lest every villager and guest alike would be tearing apart your lands and the structures upon it to join in the hunt."

"You cannot be serious." Frowning, she did not wait for him to serve her a morsel of spicy roasted duck, but speared a bit on the tip of her knife. She tested the heat of the dish by putting the bite close to her lip before nipping it off with her teeth.

"You have not guessed the object of my quest?"

Oddly, she seemed to pale at his words. What did she fear he sought? He tucked away that question to mull over another time. For now, he would share his full purpose with her, if only to draw her into the scheme and keep her quiet while he went about the task.

"I cannot possibly imagine—"

He withdrew her eating knife from her hand and set it aside, determined to serve her if only to maintain an appearance of goodwill between them.

"It is not a conversation for the hall, where anyone might overhear," he confided, choosing a steaming bit of smoked fish for her.

"There is nothing on my family lands for which you could have any rightful claim." She did not seem to see the bite of fish he waved in front of her.

There could be no doubt about it now. Her skin had lost all color.

Did she have some knowledge of the prize he sought?

"I have as much right to such a treasure as you." He kept his voice low as he replaced the food on their trencher. "It belongs with the Culcanons as much as any Domhnaill."

"It?"

He could not name the emotion behind that one incredulous word.

Cursing below his breath, he put his lips close to her ear and whispered the purpose of his quest.

"The old Viking treasure. I've discovered a reliable clue to its whereabouts."

He expected her to be pleased. The rumored wealth of a long ago mutual ancestor had been buried before a Viking invasion to protect it. But he had not antici-pated the obvious relief that sent a rush of color back into her cheeks and a burst of laughter from her lips.

"You're searching for a box of trinkets no one has discovered for some two hundred years?" The news seemed to encourage her appetite for she reached to retrieve her knife.

He clamped the jeweled handle to the table and fed her his fish offering instead. She took it without hesitation, her spirits seemingly restored as much as her appetite. By the rood, what had worried her before? What treasure had she feared he would discover at Domhnaill?

"Aye." One day he would confide how he came by the medallion with the map he wore about his neck. How his people would not make it through another winter without the spoils from such riches.

But if he could not locate the wealth of the crafty old ancestor who'd fathered both the Culcanon and Domhnaill clans long ago, claiming Cristiana's lands became all the more crucial. She might laugh at the idea of the Viking treasure, but his finding it was her only possible hope of keeping her lands. And even then? He could not imagine walking away from the strength and resources of Domhnaill. If he did not take it now, what warmongering knight might steal it out from under her? Duncan could not afford an enemy lord so close to home.

"My lady." A harried-looking young maid that

Duncan had not seen before approached Cristiana in the hall.

The maid bit her lip and frowned. Her head scarf was askew and dark curls sprang from the side as if she'd been hard at work on a difficult task.

"Yes?" Cristiana stood immediately, perhaps sensing a matter of some import.

Since the meal was well underway, he could not imagine the woman came to report any problem in the kitchen. Could the maid be a nurse to the old laird?

Duncan tensed. Not only had he liked the lord of Domhnaill, but he also found himself resenting any news that would upset Cristiana. How strange that his world had become bound up in hers again so quickly.

"You said you wished me to fetch you anytime—"

"Of course," Cristiana murmured, seizing the girl's arm as she attempted to withdraw from the table.

Duncan rose to help her, lifting her skirt to clear the bench and not receiving so much as an ill-favored look this time. But then her mind seemed elsewhere.

"I will come with you." The distracted expression upon her face concerned him.

"No!" both women exclaimed at once. The maid's eyes went to Cristiana's as if to judge her expression.

What did they hide?

"A sick room is no place for a warrior whose strength depends upon good health," Cristiana explained. "One of the children has a fever that could benefit from herbs and I'm the closest thing to a wise woman Domhnaill has. Please do enjoy the minstrels and the dancing."

Not waiting for a response, she turned on her heel and hurriedly led the maid from the hall.

Something was not right.

Thinking she would surely lead him to the old laird so he could judge her father's condition for himself, Duncan eased a narrow taper from its place on a hearthside altar and followed the women through the maze of the darkened keep.

"I think the lass sleeps, my lady," the maid told Cristiana some hours later.

Cristiana held Leah's delicate form across her lap, her niece's head cradled to her shoulder as she sang her patient a third lullaby. Her forehead no longer felt as hot, but Cristiana had not fully recovered from the scare of seeing the girl sweating and pale when she'd entered the bedchamber earlier.

Leah had found some ease, however, from a hot broth with soothing herbs.

"I don't mind holding her a bit longer," Cristiana assured her, wiping an auburn curl from Leah's forehead. "My guests have no need of me at this hour."

"Yet I did not see the young Culcanon laird bedding down in the great hall." The maid poured fresh water into a bowl by Leah's bed and folded fresh linen strips to set beside it in case the girl's skin needed more cooling in the night. "I mention it only because he seemed concerned for you earlier. Perhaps he awaits some word from you."

Cristiana did not think that was the case. But what if Duncan roamed the keep at night while everyone else slept? Was he treasure-seeking even then? Or could he be searching for something else under cover of night?

A frightening thought occurred. What if his whole tale of seeking hidden riches was, in fact, a careful fabrication intended to conceal what he really sought?

She peered down at Leah, frightened to her toes.

"Very well." Cristiana eased out from under the warm weight of the child she'd raised as her own. "I will leave her in your care, but please do have someone fetch me if the fever returns or if she seems uneasy."

"Of course." The maid rose to tuck the bed linen around Leah's shoulders. "Good night, my lady."

Fearing she'd find Duncan lurking just outside the door to the chamber, Leah shared with a nurse and two other children—an older girl who'd come to foster at Domhnaill and a boy some eight summers fathered by one of the knights, Cristiana was relieved to find the corridor clear. He had not followed her.

Unable to hasten her weary footsteps, she wound her way down the stairs of one tower and paused as she neared the great hall. All the torches had been extinguished for the night, but the hearth fire blazed as if recently stoked. Grunts and moans, giggles and sighs of couples in various stages of passion made Cristiana duck her head and hasten toward the staircase to the tower where her own bed awaited.

She nearly ran into a man and woman cavorting in the shadows outside the hall. Her feet tangled with another pair of feet, her skirts catching on the pant leg of a man who stood close to the tower stairs.

The broad, powerfully made form of the man was unmistakable even in silhouette.

"Duncan?" Righting herself, she heard a woman's soft giggle and remembered the knight was not alone.

"Cristiana." He disentwined himself from the female—a maid who worked in the kitchens—and straightened. "I've been waiting to speak with you."

"It doesn't appear to have been a hardship for you." She edged around the pair and found the stairwell. "Good eve."

"Wait." He followed her up the steps as the sound of his companion's soft footsteps disappeared into the night behind them. "We must talk privately."

Turning, she paused on the steps, hoping she did not pitch forward onto him in the dark. Why had she not brought a more substantial torch? The taper she'd taken earlier was hardly enough light to see two steps ahead of her.

"Haven't you had enough private encounters for

one day?" She gripped the rough-hewn stone wall beside her, steadying herself as she recalled that Duncan's carnal desires had never lurked far beneath the surface, even when he'd been courting her to wed. "You've made a spectacle of me already and I am not interested in your kisses, so by all means, return to a more willing partner."

A surprising amount of anger swirled through her. At him. At her. At the hapless maid who had trysted with him in a darkened corner.

"I did not wish to meet with you to make advances." His voice was harsh, guttural. Tired, perhaps? She recalled he had awakened early this day, too. "We were to discuss my quest. May I escort you to your solar? Or somewhere else that we will not be overheard?"

She'd forgotten about his treasure-hunting. In those moments in Leah's room when she'd feared he knew of the little girl's existence, she'd dismissed the quest as a pretense. Now, she wondered anew.

"My solar is no place for a male guest," she told him coldly. "Especially one who treats a woman's honor as lightly as you. Perhaps we may speak on the morrow, where our exchanges may be witnessed, if not overheard."

Wishing only to seek the safe haven of her bed and escape the constant worried churn of her thoughts, she lifted the taper high and continued her ascent.

"Then at least tell me this much." Duncan's voice

chased her through the dark even though his feet did not. "Who is the child you tended with such sweet compassion this eve?"

When she turned, Cristiana had the look of a beautiful ghost. Her eyes were wide and luminous, her skin drained of all color.

"I told you before—"

"Aye. But now I am asking who she really is. She wears the garb of a noble child. She speaks like a noble child. You held her in your arms as if—"

"You spied on us?" Oddly, her voice held more panic than anger. That, above all, stirred his suspicions.

If the girl were of no cause for concern, Cristiana would be more irritated than worried. And clearly, she was frightened.

"I had no desire to remain in the hall once you departed. By following you, I hoped to speak with you once you were free from your duties." Yet instead of dispensing a few herbs to a sick wee one and departing, Cristiana had held the child for hours.

The sight—captured in the moments he peered into the door the maid had not fully shut—had roused a protective instinct within that he had never before experienced. Seeing the maternal side of Cristiana had reminded him of all that she'd robbed him of.

Not just lands, wealth and the increased prestige

of ruling Domhnaill. He'd lost a woman who would make a strong yet tender mother.

He swore under his breath. He did not owe her any sympathy. If he was right about the little girl she hid, then Cristiana had deceived him as thoroughly as he tricked her with his pretense for entering her keep.

"What is it?" Her voice was a thin wisp of sound in the drafty tower staircase.

"*You* are her mother." The realization hit him like a rockslide.

They stared at one another, locked in wordless indictment. A myriad of emotions passed over her features. Did she think to deny it? Her long delay as good as confirmed his suspicions.

"Do not think about lying to me," he warned.

"It is true. She is mine." She gave a tight nod, her lips pressed in a flat line.

Yet, she appeared relieved at the same time. As if there were a great weight off her shoulders now that she'd shared the truth.

Anger welled up in him as though a jealous fist squeezed his insides.

"She is not yet five summers, but she is close. What knave dared to touch you while you yet belonged to me?" He closed the distance between them, gaze locked upon her. He should not care if she'd taken a lover back then. Until that day that he'd kissed her by the wishing well, he'd paid her little enough attention, agreeing to the betrothal out of a sense of duty.

He'd had a lover of his own, after all. But that was not the same and she knew it. He would hunt down the man who'd touched her.

"No one, I swear it." She shook her head, as if the idea were repugnant. "I would die before forswearing myself."

The vehemence in her words was so powerful, so passionate. Could they be true?

"Then when did it happen?" His chest was tight with fury. He would have never guessed proud Cristiana would defile herself that way. And yet, he'd seen the girl. The cinnamon curls and delicate shape of her face mirrored the Domhnaill women exactly.

"It was that summer after you and your brother departed. I—I was devastated." Her voice lowered. Softened. "I did not ever wish to wed after what happened."

The thought of her touching another man so soon after he'd kissed her sent a maelstrom of violent emotion through him. His breathing possessed the ragged harshness of a man who'd fought a days-long battle.

It should not affect him so much. But by all that was holy, the child she tended should have been his. Anger and possessiveness tightened around him, choking him.

"Yet you could not deny yourself passion. Passion that I introduced you to. Passion that should have been mine to claim." He couldn't have hidden the fierceness in his voice if he tried.

She backed up a step, but she must have caught her heel on her hem for she stumbled and pitched forward. Her flickering taper fell from her hand and tumbled down the stairs, the light extinguishing as the beeswax column rolled away.

"Oh!"

Catching her in his arms, Duncan was in no mood to tread lightly around her anymore. She was no maid to deny his kiss and deny herself womanly pleasure. She had run to another man and gladly tasted passion after she'd cast him aside.

He would not let her rebuff him again.

Wrapping an arm about her back, he sealed her breasts to his chest. Her rapidly beating heart aligned with the thunderous throb of his. Not giving her any quarter, he picked up where they'd left off in the brew house. Threading a hand through her hair, he tipped her head back and found her mouth with his.

Darkness enveloped them, cocooning them in a world lit only by fiery need. He backed her against the wall, protecting her back from the hard stone by sacrificing his knuckles to the unforgiving granite. While one hand cradled her head, his other pressed her hips into his.

She made a muffled cry that could have been plea-sure or pain, but she did not attempt to free herself. If anything, her mouth relaxed under the pressure of his, her back arching so that her breasts tested the neckline of her dress. He could feel velvet and linen shifting beneath his onslaught, the beaded crests of her womanly curves an undeniable sign that she was not just a curious maid anymore, but a woman in need of his touch.

With a tug and a yank, he wrenched free the tie that laced her gown up one side. Velvet slithered from her shoulders, leaving her warm, creamy skin protected by naught but frail linen that was no match for him.

He kissed his way down her neck, savoring stolen tastes of her fragrant skin as he neared her collarbone. Her shoulder. The swell of her breast.

As his mouth closed around one tight bud, she cried out. Her fingers closed around his tunic, clenching and opening again and again as he drew her deep into his mouth. Had her first lover given her such pleasure?

Protest shuddered through him and his only defense was to pleasure her better. More. Drive the bastard who'd stolen her innocence from her head forever.

He released her flesh and lifted her off her feet, careful of her head near the stone wall. His heart thundered in his ears as their breathing echoed in the winding tower.

"I'm taking you to your bed." He climbed the steps, cradling her close to his body. And while he could not see her features clearly in the shadowed tower with only a few arrow slits to spill scant winter moonlight, he could picture the way she looked right now.

Her auburn hair spilling over his arm to cloak his shoulder. Her skin pink and damp from his kisses.

Her calves exposed by her skirts, waiting for more thorough exploration.

"Nay." Her whispered word was all but drowned out by his pounding footfalls up the steps. "We must not."

"You. Belonged. To. Me." Each word coincided with the hard stomp of a boot impressing his will as he reached the gallery at last. "I never betrayed you. I did nothing to earn your enmity."

The full import of her perfidy—denying his marriage contract while offering herself freely to another man—was a newly ripped wound that would not heal without some concession on her part. An admission of how wrong she'd been. A confession that it had been *him* she'd wanted and not some black-hearted knave who gave her nothing.

"You allowed us to think your half brother was as much a Culcanon as you."

The cold words slowed his step as he reached a door that he could only assume led to her chamber. The outer towers of Domhnaill were narrow, each housing naught but storage for arms and a chamber.

"He is my father's son." Duncan had never begrudged his half brother his rightful share of the legacy that would be theirs. "Half of Culcanon belongs to Malcolm."

"But I have heard he has tried to steal the whole

of it for himself while you did your king's bidding in foreign lands. No Culcanon worthy of the name would undermine his own blood. I cannot believe you did not know that a traitorous heart beat within him when you came to Domhnaill in search of brides."

The icy venom in her voice reached through his anger. The fury was still there, but he had to put it aside long enough to make sense of this new accusation.

"It is true Malcolm tried to seize control while I was away. He has changed since your sister refused him. Bitterness can ruin a man." He gazed down into Cristiana's eyes, now visible by the small torch someone had left alight at her door. "Indeed, I know its sting tonight more strongly than ever before."

The powerful emotions that burned inside him clamored for release. Demanded an answer for her faithlessness.

Yet when she twisted in his arms, he knew he would never find satisfaction in imposing his will upon a woman he'd once vowed to honor. No matter that the oath had not been sworn in front of a priest. He had promised as much to her in the kisses they'd shared.

"Release me," she demanded, perhaps not realizing how the urgent writhing of her body only reminded him how quickly he could turn her anger to something far more enjoyable for them both.

With regret, he lowered her to her feet.

"I will not take in anger what you won't give freely," he promised. But that did not mean he would let the matter drop. "Know this, however. I will not treat you like an innocent maid any longer. You are a woman with earthy experience and I will not forget it. The next time we meet in an abandoned corridor, have a care. When I touch you again, I will apply every last skill to make you beg me for more."

She opened her mouth to speak, then snapped it shut again. With a shaky little nod, she acknowledged his warning and fled into her chamber.

He was not surprised to hear the bar lower across the door on the other side.

Edwina of Domhnaill was no stranger to heart-break.

Although she had put hers firmly in her past, she lived through other people's enough times that she had a good nose for sensing when trouble was on the horizon. Right now, listening to the careless whispers of rebellion on the villagers' lips while she shopped in the small market at Evesburh, she could almost feel the inevitable despair of these poor souls foolish enough to rebel against the rule of her overlord, William the Bastard.

Or, the Conqueror, as his biographers now preferred he be called. No matter the name, Edwina respected the king's indomitable strength. It was underestimated by the churls wolfing down meat pies near the empty village stocks at this small hamlet outside Northumbria. But Edwina had not made the mistake of underestimating a strong man ever since Donegal the Crude—a name of her own making— had deceived her into thinking he would wed her and then seduced her.

Brutalized her.

"Edwina."

The deep male voice behind her was obvious enough to identify, but she pretended not to recognize it in order to draw out her latest suitor.

"Who would speak my Christian name in public without regard to my reputation?" Closing her eyes, she tapped her finger to her lips thoughtfully.

She'd been sent on a short errand for a local noble-woman, one of the countless fortunate Normans who had inherited the country since the debacle at Hastings. Edwina had been instructed to seek good herbs to make fresh dyes for the lady's embroidery thread.

"My lady." The man behind her lowered his voice, bending closer to be heard. "I meant no offense."

"Yes, Henry, but I keep hoping one day you will," she teased, spinning on her heel to face him. She opened her eyes and feigned delight at his young, pockmarked visage.

Henry Osgood would have been a handsome enough youth, but childhood disease had not been kind to him. Edwina admired his warrior's strength, however, even if he was not exceedingly clever. Actually, that thick wit of his worked in her favor, since he had no ear for the nuances of court gossip and resolutely refused to listen to anyone speak unkindly of her.

A first.

Since her arrival in King William's court four years ago as an exile—and a ruined one at that—she had often been the subject of suggestive rumor. No one knew for certain about her past, but the fact that she kept it well hidden spoke volumes. Only Edwina knew of the child she bore. The child she'd given up so that the little girl would have a better life. Even thinking of it now caused her heart to tighten and ache.

But it had been for the best. Her sister would take care of Leah and protect her from the gossip that would hound Edwina forever. Instead of letting life defeat her, she'd become a bit of a warrior herself, making herself useful to anyone who could put her in a position to return home.

Calculating her next move, she turned back to the bins of fresh herbs she'd been culling through before he arrived, seeking out the leaves and stems with the strongest scents and richest colors.

"You are too cruel to remind me of your idle fancies when they cut me to the quick." She took an odd pride in her skill at manipulating men and sometimes she found herself down on her knees in church to beg forgiveness for it. But then, she'd never been able to forgive her attacker for what he'd done to her. And each man she maneuvered into giving her what she wanted soothed an old wound she doubted would ever heal.

Not every man would have been taken in by such obvious guile, but Edwina considered that part of her gift. She understood which men could be duped by this method, and which men required cunning or directness.

"How so?" Henry touched her shoulder in order to encourage her gaze. A caress which he withdrew almost immediately.

She knew she had a powerful effect upon him.

"Please, do not," she entreated him sweetly, rubbing her fingers meaningfully over the place he had just touched, as if that brush of his hand were a caress she'd craved. "You know I will not wed while I am in exile. I must return home. No woman wants to speak her vows in a strange land among people who do not care about her. Have you so little concern for my future?"

Or her dowry?

She did not speak the thought aloud, however, knowing Henry's noble soul would be wounded all over again at the suggestion.

Around them, spice traders and bakers, metalworkers and weavers began to pack their wares to close the market stalls by noon.

"It means so much to you?" Henry pressed, removing

two pouches of herbs from her hand so that she could rummage through the remaining bins. Unencumbered. "Enough to risk our safety?"

"Domhnaill is on the water, so you needn't travel on dangerous roads." If he waited for the land passages to clear, she would be stuck here until the end of spring. "Now that the Danes have given up on the coast, the sea is very safe for travelers."

She had turned toward him in her excitement and for a moment, she thought he considered it. But then he let out a ripe bark of laughter and handed back her herbs.

"Edwina, those eyes of yours are enough to drive a man to almost consider it." He grinned and shook his head. "I will wait until you come to your senses. But I *will* wait for you, my sweet."

His tender words didn't begin to penetrate her cold anger, but she did her best to appear only mildly miffed. She would need Henry and his protection yet. How else would she return to Domhnaill without her father's approval or her own coin?

Soon, she would slip out of her bed one night and put her wiles to work. Poor Henry's honor was about to be tested to the fullest.

Chapter Five

❦

"I don't know why I have to wait with you," Keane grumbled later that week as he stood beside Cristiana in the great hall. "Can you not wait for the young Culcanon and bring him to your da's chamber when he arrives?"

"No." She gripped the old adviser's wrist, unwilling to meet Duncan alone for even a moment.

Although he'd been a gentleman the past three days, she had not dismissed the warning he'd given her outside her chamber. She would not be foolish enough to tempt fate and cross paths with him unaccompanied. In the past, she'd been sorely tempted by his stolen kisses. How great might the allure become if he applied all his efforts toward seduction?

She was ashamed to admit how much time she had devoted toward considering the topic. Her body still burned with the memory of what had happened on the staircase leading to her chamber.

"Well, I don't know how you expect your da to scare off the man when the laird has not been reminded what you hope to gain from this meeting." Keane scrubbed the matted fur atop one of the hounds' heads as the older man paced in front of the hearth. "He gets confused. He will not know to let me do the talking."

They had already moved the appointment once, as the laird had been particularly unwell the day they first intended to speak. Cristiana had begged Keane to send Duncan a note using her father's seal, since she had not wanted to broach the topic with him herself. She had decided her safest course of action was to keep her distance and do whatever she could to encourage a speedy leave-taking.

"I went to his chamber earlier to remind him." Cristiana had not let her father forget that a Culcanon touched Edwina without the protection of marriage. And while her father did not know about the babe that resulted from the union, he had stormed about the keep threatening war for days afterward. Cristiana felt certain he would recall their enmity for a few hours at least. "He knows we hope do drive Duncan away and get back to the business of choosing a viable successor to—"

"My lady. Keane." Duncan's low tone rolled through the hall, his voice touching a nerve with her. He stood in the door and gave a shallow bow in greeting. His high color and damp hair gave him the appearance of a man who'd already been out of doors. "Shall we?"

Keane gave the hound a last scratch and hurried over.

"Aye." The word croaked from her lips as if she hadn't spoken in a sennight. She'd been silent beside him at sup the past few days, eating quickly and then rising from her seat to make merry with other guests.

Keane did not seem to notice any awkwardness, however. He hurried toward the doors while the matted hound barked at his retreat.

"This way, then." He waved Duncan to follow him. "The laird expects us, but he has much to do today and will not have a great deal of time."

Cristiana heard the nervousness in the counselor's voice as they sought the back stairs leading directly from the hall to the laird's chamber. Would Duncan detect the anxiousness, too?

For the first time, Cristiana saw her household as Duncan might—ruled by frail men aided by a woman. Up until that time, she had allowed herself to believe that Domhnaill's strong walls, legendary wealth and generosity would preserve them until another member of the clan took over as laird. But what if their weakness showed all too clearly?

Might Duncan truly take the keep in the king's name?

She wished more than ever that she had not allowed this meeting.

"My message for the laird will not take long to deliver." Duncan's clipped response gave her scant assurance.

What if he merely wanted to convey his intention to claim Domhnaill? He'd threatened as much that day back in the brew house, but she had not taken him seriously.

"Duncan, wait." She paused just outside her father's rooms.

But her former betrothed never slowed his pace. Instead, he rapped upon the door guarded by a lone man-at-arms.

"Wait? Your adviser has just suggested we move things along in a timely manner. Let us see your father while we can. You and I can talk later." His expression shifted as his eyes darkened. "Perhaps we can finally speak privately?"

His voice hummed along her senses, alerting her to the warning and the invitation that came hand in hand with his offer. She hated that her heart beat faster, knowing she had more to fear from her own weakness than from him. He'd proven to her three nights ago that he was a man of great restraint and nothing like his brother.

But that deep sense of honor of his that put her innocence in her own hands, was the same sort of honor that would never abide keeping Leah from her father.

"We can go right in," Keane assured them, peering back and forth between them as if he could make sense of the undercurrents if given enough time.

Cristiana did not think even she could understand what forces were at work between her and Duncan, so as crafty as her father's adviser was, she did not worry that he would guess the full import of their exchange.

Keane opened the door, leading the way into her father's rooms. Cristiana followed quickly, edging past Duncan as he held the door. Even that brief moment of nearness was enough to stir her senses. The warmth of his powerful body called to mind those moments in his arms when he'd carried her to her chamber. The pine and leather scent of him reminded her how much time he spent outdoors, a strong presence on Domhnaill lands even though he did not lead the people.

Sweet merciful heaven. What if he'd been riding the perimeter of the lands all this sennight to take full measure of the property he planned to seize?

"I never thought I would see a Culcanon dare to return to my keep," her father said by way of greeting, calling her from fearful thoughts.

Sensing more fight in him than she had seen in some time, Cristiana felt hope stir. She moved to take a seat on one side of him while Keane ambled over to the other. The laird's chamber was a wide, long room that had once housed the whole family while the towers were being constructed. The extra space now held a table where the laird could conduct his affairs or meet with advisers privately. Duncan claimed a seat across the wide table from them.

"And I never thought I would see one of the strongest lairds in the kingdom allow his keep to go underdefended for so long." Duncan planted his forearms on the table and leaned across it. "Are you trying to invite war? Even across the border in King William's court, they say Domhnaill is ripe for plucking."

Keane rose to his feet, incensed to his Highland toes at the notion. But beside her, her da appeared confused again.

"They say that?" He shook his head, shaggy eyebrows drawn together. "I have enough gold to pay the men-at-arms on these walls for well nigh two years."

"But you've no one to lead them. And you know as well as I that paid men are only as loyal as their next coin when there is no strong leader to guide them."

"We will make a transition soon," Keane assured him. "This is why you wanted to meet with the laird? To insult his rule when your own keep falls about your ears in your absence? We have all heard that thieving brother of yours has stolen from you the same way he stole from us five years ago."

Cristiana tensed, confused by Keane's seeming attack on Duncan now when the adviser had all but championed him a week ago to take over Domhnaill. Had the older man recovered his sense? Or were his accusations a kind of political maneuvering? If only her father had maintained his wits, she would have trusted his judgment completely.

"Edwina would not even meet with us to make her accusation," Duncan reminded him. "We had no reason to believe her over Donegal."

Cristiana bit her lip hard to keep from entering the discussion. It would do no good to berate the half brother now. But how dare Duncan suggest Edwina should have displayed private bruises in intimate places as testament to her word?

Keane sank back to his seat.

"Aye. You had no reason to discount your brother's word back then. What about now? Do you think maybe you were a wee bit hasty to take up for the knave now that you've witnessed his treachery firsthand?"

"I am willing to concede that Edwina was wronged." Duncan did not look at her. Did not allude to the fact that he had told Cristiana quite the opposite very recently.

"Wait a moment—" She did not like the sound of a conversation that resembled a negotiation.

"You have the goodwill of the king?" her father asked, his eyes showing the shrewdness that used to be there all the time and now only came in fits and starts.

"I served him well overseas. He would give me

Culcanon outright, but I do not wish war on my people. I will wrest my share from Donegal. 'Tis Domhnaill that is to be my prize."

The announcement hit her like a blow.

"No." She studied his features, searching for some hint that he fabricated the news. "You came to the gates to seek shelter. I only admitted you for charity's sake."

"I hoped to speak to your father peaceably and spare your people any undue fear. I have seen first-hand at Culcanon how quickly loyalties divide when the villagers are frightened."

She could scarcely absorb his words. For the past three days, she'd been so cautious around him, biding her time until he left, so that her world could return to normal. When all along he'd known that she was to be deposed and he was the one who would rule here.

A Culcanon was to inherit the Domhnaill legacy after all, no matter her vow to her sister.

"You've shown us mercy," her father admitted, though there was a weariness to his voice that broke her heart. "Perhaps, now that you've seen the error of your trust in Donegal, you will show us one more bit of mercy."

"I think we can all agree I've been patient already." Duncan stood, his large frame unfurling from the bench to loom over them. "We will make an announcement to the guests at sup tonight before everyone departs on the morrow."

"Just consider one more bit of generosity toward the people of Domhnaill, as their goodwill toward you ensures their loyalty," her father pressed. He rose to his feet now, too, though he leaned heavily upon the table to do so. Still, the old warrior was near as tall as Duncan, and would have been if old injuries had not bowed his back.

"Sir, do not ask it," Duncan warned, perhaps guessing what "mercy" her father wanted him to show.

Cristiana, perhaps distracted by the many ways this news would alter her life forever, did not anticipate the old laird's request.

"Take my daughter." He shook a finger in Duncan's face. "Wed Cristiana as you once intended and you will win more acceptance here than any show of strength or contract from a king could ever garner."

"Never." It was her turn to rise. There was no way she would accept such a proposition. To do so could endanger Leah. "I might be able to bend my knee to a new laird, and leave behind every bit of the life I've known. But do not ask me to speak vows that would bind me to a false-tongued knave who played upon my sympathies for entrance to the keep and who lied about his purpose here every day. I will not do it."

The lady of the keep might not believe him. But since his arrival at Domhnaill, Duncan had been true to his word. He had, for example, shared small treasures with Cristiana and her people each night at sup.

After the kiss he'd given her that first day—his most enjoyable discovery by far—he'd presented her with garlands of holly to decorate her hall, a sack full of pheasants for a saint's day feast and an exotic songbird he'd captured at great risk to life and limb in the hopes that she would delight in its unusual song.

No gift had been particularly well received. Although there'd been a moment during that kiss when he'd thought maybe…

But she'd remained unmoved to the point where she would not even consider a marriage she'd once been most eager to accept. He ruminated over the rejection that day as he worked with his men in a young field of fruit trees to hone their skills after sitting idle for a sennight. Duncan had recovered their weapons after his talk with the old laird, assuring the man he had no intention of using force upon the men-at-arms currently employed on the walls for protection. Duncan planned to keep them on, in fact, but until he'd announced his assumption of the stronghold to the people, he kept his men's swordplay far from the keep.

If Cristiana discovered his intentions, there would be no more enticing kisses. And truth be told, he wanted the taste of her on his lips again.

"You won the rights to the place with no bloodshed and no bride." Rory the Lothian met a charge from Duncan's sword with his shield, the reverberation jarring him to his teeth.

"He puts much stock in the fact that I have served the king." Duncan had not exaggerated Malcolm's promise of both coastal keeps. But he had no writ or deed to that end as Malcolm would have never committed armed forces to secure lands Duncan should be able to claim on his own.

But Duncan had put himself in an untenable situation by not conquering the keep with the sword. Out of respect for Cristiana and her people, he'd opted to keep them all safe. Of course, that meant he'd resorted to an even sharper weapon.

A cunning she would not appreciate when she found out.

"What of the lass?" Rory whipped the sword at knee-level, driving Duncan backward into a tree branch.

It was the memory of his time with Cristiana that had him fighting like a squire instead of a seasoned warrior. Plunging forward, he forced Rory's blade aside, accomplishing by brute strength what he could not with strategy.

Perhaps he'd tapped all of his shrewdness in his battle with Cristiana.

"She does not wish to wed." He shoved his friend aside, sweating from the practice battle despite the cold wind blowing in from the sea and the hard-packed snow beneath their feet.

"I do not ask what she wishes." Rory swung his sword in an arc over his head and then swapped the haft to the other hand to repeat the motion. "What is to become of her? Will you send her off to live with far-off kin or allow her to remain on your lands? Would you benefit from a marriage between her and one of your men?"

Duncan stilled. His gaze flew to the other knight's face, but the man was engrossed in wearing himself out with the blade, engaging an invisible foe in battle.

"What are you asking?" Possessiveness roiled inside him like a great beast stirred to life. "Do you suggest I hand her over to you?"

Rory glanced up from his sword work.

"You don't want a deposed heiress marrying a powerful enemy who will use his claim to her as a claim to Domhnaill." His gaze never wavered as he seemed to take Duncan's measure. "Far better to bind her to someone who is loyal to you. Someone less powerful."

"You want her." The realization did nothing to soothe the beast in his chest. The fresh snow falling all around them did not cool a temper quickly rising. "You have sat in her hall and watched her. Coveted her."

The thought of his friend's hands upon Cristiana

made a vein throb in his temple. A dark storm of fury swirled in his gut.

"I offer to relieve you of a potential burden and retain the most skilled mead maker in the land." Rory's gaze narrowed. "But I would not propose it if I found the prospect of having her unappealing."

His temple pounded harder now.

"She does not wish to wed." He recalled her declaration vividly. She'd been so adamantly opposed to her father's suggestion that she had walked out of his chamber at the mere mention of such a union.

As if she could yet make some lofty marriage when she was not even a maid.

"She is a noblewoman of an important family. She has no choice."

The knight's tone was so reasonable that some of Duncan's anger ebbed. For all that he did not appreciate another man thinking about Cristiana in a wifely manner, he could respect the practicality of Rory's strategy.

He made a good point about her becoming a threat if she wed someone with an eye to claim Domhnaill.

"Her father wants me to take her to wife." He had gone over and over that conversation in his mind, recalling with disturbing clarity the jolt that had gone through him at the suggestion.

"That makes the most sense. But if you do not desire her—"

"I do." The words echoed with fierce truth. "I did not recall how much until we returned to her lands."

He had been young when she'd broken their betrothal. He had regretted it, but he'd found other women to console himself with. The fact that she'd found another man had been a visceral blow he would never have expected.

Could he trust her now? Could he trust himself to raise another man's child with a merciful heart? He was unsure. But the desire for her— Ah, that had never been an issue. He wanted her more than he'd ever wanted any woman.

"Then you have more to recommend this union than most men." Rory sheathed his sword, perhaps recognizing when to concede. "Do not allow your pride—or hers—to dissuade you from the best course for Domhnaill. A prize such as this is worth great sacrifice."

As Rory's boots crunched through the hard snow on his way back to the keep, Duncan's gaze swept the landscape. It was a magnificent keep, with a thriving village. It had been home to his ancestors, as well as Cristiana's, given that the lands were once united under one banner.

He would claim the Domhnaill lands along with its heiress. She would be safest with him. And while she might not be the same innocent lass he'd kissed in the gardens five years ago, she was a woman whose passions would warm him on the cold winter nights.

But just as he would do no harm to the lands and her people when he claimed them, he would not push Cristiana to wed until she came to him of her own will.

He'd been so close to having her three nights ago, back when he'd been playing fair where she was concerned. Now, the stakes were higher. He could not afford to give her occasion to reason and rethink and demur when hot desire surfaced.

Next time, he would answer her hunger in full measure. He would drive them both to the brink before it ever occurred to her he might be playing for keeps.

Chapter Six

"Mother, come play."

Cristiana looked up from the letter she labored over to see Leah stacking a pile of flat stones in the corner of her solar. The sweet endearment of "Mother" had not been discouraged, the honorary designation one of Leah's choosing at an early age. If the servants thought if peculiar she shared such a bond with an orphaned noble child they said naught.

Now a day had passed since Cristiana's world had been rocked to the core by the revelation of a takeover approved by the king. In the course of an afternoon, she'd not only lost her standing as mistress of Domhnaill, but she'd also managed to break an oath to her sister. By failing to find a new laird to take her father's place sooner, she'd allowed the keep to appear ripe for the taking.

"I must finish a letter to your aunt," she began, but as she stared at the parchment with scarcely a mark upon it, she had to admit she was accomplishing little. "Though, perhaps I could take a short break."

Rising from her seat at a writing table that accounted for the chamber's only furnishing aside from two chairs, Cristiana joined Leah on the floor near the hearth. Edwina's daughter—actually, *Cristiana's* daughter in the ways that counted—had recovered quickly from her fever earlier in the week. Still, she'd kept the girl close to watch over her personally.

She was so proud of Leah. A fierce heart lurked inside the child's delicate form. She'd come into the world shrieking and waving tiny fists, and in four years' time she'd learned much about bending the world to her will. Cristiana tried not to indulge her overmuch, but it was difficult not to smile privately over the child's quick mind and talent for winning her own way. Even the older children admired her and followed where she led.

"What are we playing?" Cristiana asked, grateful for the diversion from dark thoughts that had chased around her brain all night and day.

She had no idea how she would face her guests on what would be the last night at Domhnaill for most. How could she sit beside Duncan while he announced his rule? Then again, perhaps she would not even have the option of sitting at the high table now. She might arrive in the great hall to find the silk curtains behind the laird's seat had been replaced with Duncan's banner.

"We are defending our fortress," Leah told her solemnly, her green eyes fixed on the pile of stones on the floor surrounded by intermittent rocks in a ring around it. She held a stick in her hand and seemed to be breaking off pieces to set between the rocks. "The twigs are my men and they defend the walls. I am king and you can be my squire."

Leah handed her the stick, her long auburn curls covering her shoulders. She took after Cristiana more than Edwina, both in her hair color and the shape of her face. They even shared the same mannerisms. Cristiana still found it unnerving to watch Leah stir her small cauldron of mead in the brew house on the days she was allowed to work beside her. The child stirred three times clockwise and three times counter clockwise, just as she did.

"I am the squire?" Cristiana accepted the thin branch that rustled with a handful of stubborn, disintegrating leaves still attached.

"Yes." Leah folded her arms and stuck out her bottom lip, appearing every inch the petulant monarch. "You must do my bidding."

Cristiana studied her child, so very serious in her role. With her circlet askew and her one veil slipping down her shoulder, Leah had the look of a girl at play. But her tilted chin and clear-eyed certainty about the roles in this game made Cristiana all the more fearful of the situation she had put them both in.

By keeping faith with Edwina—fighting against Duncan's rule—Cristiana could take pride in her loyalty to family. But would it be at Leah's expense? Why should Leah lose what tenuous standing she had as an illegitimate child of the nobility to become just another fatherless little girl? Leah's future was tied to the decisions Cristiana made now.

"I will do my best, sire," she played along, taking the branch and snapping off more pieces to serve as men-at-arms on the make-believe castle walls. "But the forces below are swelling. I do not know if we can hold them off."

Her voice caught on the words, her heart heavy with the weight of responsibility. Her love for Leah—her duty to raise her well—stirred something fiercely maternal within her breast.

"Domhnaill is the strongest keep in the east!" she cried, the defiant set to her jaw reminding Cristiana of her father. "We will not know defeat."

Her hands paused on the branch, her fingers slowing in their work.

"How are you so sure, my sweet?" She set aside the long stick, savoring the feel of the hearth fire on her back and the chance to be with Leah. For two weeks, she'd been avoiding her own daughter in a need to make everything appear as normal as possible. The less anyone noticed Leah, the less chance anyone questioned her identity.

Or remarked on the striking resemblance between her soft green eyes and the mossy hue that belonged to all the Culcanons.

"We throw fire at them," Leah whispered as she bent over her game, her cinnamon curls spilling on the floor and blanketing the pretend keep. "And dump chamber pots on their heads. Cook says she can boil water to scald a whole band of beetle-brained thievin' invaders."

Cristiana knew Leah occasionally spent time in the kitchens with the other children, eating an extra meal early in the day to fill their smaller bellies. Clearly the conversation had caught Leah's imagination.

Still, how was it the child had gone from cooing babe to battle strategist overnight?

"I remember." Cristiana had been little more than a child. The skirmish had been one of the reasons her father wished to unite the family with Duncan's—their combined forces would have been formidable. "I was very frightened when that happened."

The memory reminded her that Duncan's bloodless takeover—while devastating in its own way—at least spared her people the gut-churning fear of death and ruin at the hands of barbarous invading forces.

"You were scared?" Leah straightened, staring at Cristiana in disbelief. "*I* would not have been scared.

I would take the laird's sword and ram it through anyone who scaled the walls!"

She acted out the motion with the authenticity of a child who'd watched the knights practice often enough.

"Well, you are much braver than me," she told her, unsettled at her daughter's pledge of vigorous defense, even though Leah was far too young to understand they'd already lost Domhnaill to another kind of invader.

The faithless, lying kind.

"Domhnaill is home," Leah explained simply, brushing her long hair from her eyes impatiently. "We brave much to protect it."

With that, Leah snuggled closer to her, peering up at Cristiana with the kind of adoring, trusting smile that could pierce a mother's heart. Content that all was right with her world, the child picked up the branch again to continue populating the pretend keep with armed guards.

Leah expected her family to fight for their home at any cost. And while the view might be childish and naive considering the circumstances, it was one many others shared. Cristiana had overheard unrest and discontent among her highest-ranking advisers ever since Duncan had arrived.

"You're right, sweeting." She stroked Leah's hair while the child struggled to break a stubborn piece of the branch, her movements slowing as she grew tired.

"We would all be very brave if we had to protect our family legacy."

In that moment, she knew boiling water to scald the new laird was not an option. There was far more at stake here than a keep. Something more important than lands and men. And Cristiana planned to fight as hard to protect her daughter as Leah battled her imaginary war.

She only hoped Edwina would forgive her for the sacrifice she would have to make to see Leah safely installed at Domhnaill forever.

"You want to marry who?" Keane and her father stared at her in equal disbelief, their expressions mirrored images of one another.

Cristiana sat across from them in her brew house before sup. Keane insisted on providing the laird with fresh air and exercise every day, escorting him about the grounds when the activity in the keep was at a minimum. They had entered the brew house merely for a cup of mead, but Cristiana hoped she could win them over prior to an announcement that Duncan would become laird. She knew he planned to claim the keep as his before her holiday guests departed, effectively spreading his fame far and wide as the visiting nobles rode back to their far-flung lands.

If her plan to protect Leah and secure her within Domhnaill's walls forever was to work, Cristiana needed to counteract Duncan's announcement immediately.

"Sir Cullen of Blackstone." She took pride in the fact that she said the name without hesitation. Cullen was a guest in residence and could easily be named laird of Domhnaill instead of Duncan.

A strong knight in his prime, Cullen was without a wife and had offered for Edwina long before her betrothal to Donegal, though Cullen's suit had been overlooked at the time because he could not meet the bride price. But he had more lands and men now, his star having risen in the world. Surely one Domhnaill daughter was as good as the next?

"Daughter." Her father shook his head, his wrinkled brow making him look forlorn and confused. "You speak of a man far older than you. He was older than Edwina, and Edwina has several summers upon you."

Keane rummaged in a cupboard and emerged with the largest drinking horn to be found in the brew house.

"Don't forget, lass, this is the same man you called a dried-up weevil and far worse, back when the poor man offered for your sister." Keane took his bandy-legged stride about the perimeter of the large, open chamber, peering into the various cauldrons contents. "Do you think he's improved with age? And how can you think he would defend these walls with as much vigor as Duncan the Brave?"

Ah, she'd been a fool back then, not seeing beyond the surface of Cullen. He was a nice enough man. And he'd hardly been a dried-up weevil seven summers ago.

"You'll want children," her father said softly, touching her heart with the way his cloudy gaze seemed to see into a future already full of grandsons and granddaughters. "And the seed of a younger man is more vital."

Keane must have found a cauldron of mead that pleased him for he dunked his cup into one without a care for the fact that it was nowhere near ready to drink.

"Aye." Keane raised his vessel with the enthusiasm of a young knight toasting his overlord. "Here's to vigor in the bedchamber."

"My lord father," she intoned urgently, appealing to the more probable source of relenting. "I would not be forced to wed a man not of my choosing and you know there is much bad blood between our family and the Culcanons—"

Her father nodded and tucked her under one heavy arm. The gesture reminded her of happier days when they had walked and talked together in her youth, back when her father had been the most powerful man she could imagine.

"There is no such thing as bad blood, Crissie." He shook a finger under his nose, his signet ring loose upon one digit now that he'd lost weight and youth. "Just look at Leah."

She stilled, everything inside her growing cold despite the hot fire warming the room. Had her father guessed Leah's true parentage? Did those rheumy eyes see more than anyone knew?

"I do not understand."

"The girl is an orphan of unknown origin. Yet you raise her to be as clever and sweetly mannered as you were yourself when you were a wee tot. She is not of noble blood, but we would hardly say she has bad blood, would we?"

Cristiana studied her father in the fragrant, smoky brew house, trying to find some hint that he was telling her he knew her secret. But he merely smiled and patted her shoulder as he released her.

"So I do not believe in bad blood. I believe in good alliances and second chances. Duncan has pleased our king, so let us not see if he can please you. Nothing would make me happier than to know you were installed as lady here for the rest of your days."

Panic swelled in her belly. It did not stem from the dishonor she would do to her sister. What would Duncan say when he learned that she was a maid after all? He was a smart man. He knew the season of Leah's birth and he would guess her heritage.

It would only be a matter of time before Donegal would arrive and take Leah away forever.

"I can be lady of Domhnaill with Cullen at my

side," she insisted, already quaking at the thought of being separated from Leah. And again, there was a twinge of wistfulness over the passion she'd felt for Duncan. She would never know such feelings with any other man. "If you will not ask him to consider me as a bride, I will ask him myself."

"What?" Keane perked up from the cup of mead he had fairly lost himself in.

But Cristiana did not remain to listen to his protests or her father's. No matter that she would never know true passion, she needed to act quickly to thwart the one man who could ruin everything she'd worked so hard to safeguard.

No one knew where Cristiana had gone.

Duncan had asked maids and knights, squires and ladies as the day grew late and the last night of holiday merriment approached. He stalked a gallery deserted of the noble company who normally slept there, dodging the servants who loaded their overlords' belongings into chests for the next day's travel. Only one chamber door was closed and Duncan approached it, wishing to be sure Cristiana was not anywhere in the main keep before he started searching for her in one of the outlying buildings.

She was probably in the brew house. Yet an uneasy feeling had been crawling up his neck ever since Rory mentioned what a valuable bride a Domhnaill daughter would make. Duncan had not thought through her future well enough, somehow assuming she would remain here in one capacity or another, since her father was here. Her people were here.

Besides, Cristiana had vowed not to wed. But since when did noble women have the right to exercise such an option? He'd been a fool to think she would remain under his roof once he became laird.

The longer his deceit went undetected, the more difficult it would be to untwine himself from the truth of his arrival here.

"Cristiana," he said her name through the heavy door, rapping on the hardwood with his knuckles. "Are you in there?"

He was about to leave when he heard a small sound from within the chamber. A soft cry?

Not the sweet, womanly sound of a feminine passion. Nay, the noise he'd detected was more of a muffled sob.

"Cristiana?" He knocked upon the door with new urgency. Hearing no response, he tried the handle and discovered the barrier had been bolted from within. "Who's in there?"

Not waiting for a reply, he applied his shoulder to the plank boards. Perhaps he would only find an unhappy lady whose husband had gone down to sup without her. But his gut said otherwise.

"Sir?" a maid approached him while he pounded at the polished oak door.

"Aye?" He did not even let up for a moment.

"Shall I retrieve the laird or Lady Cristiana?" the young woman raised her voice to be heard over the creak and groan of the wood that protested his efforts.

But just then, there was a metallic "clink" and the sound of wood and metal scraping together on the other side of the door.

Both Duncan and the maid paused to stare until the door creaked open.

Lady Cristiana herself stood within. He could not see much of her through the narrow opening. A hint of deep saffron surcoat and creamy kirtle. Pale cheeks and stormy gray eyes rimmed with red.

Perhaps sensing the high tension that crackled to life, the maid dipped a curtsy and disappeared into a nearby chamber.

If Duncan had imagined any tender words or a conciliatory approach for this moment, the intent fled at the sight of her. She'd hidden from him purposely. And, for the love of heaven, was she in another man's quarters?

An empty pallet lay in one corner, the rushes disturbed enough to make him think someone had slept there recently.

"What are you doing?" He stalked inside, his hands twitching with the need to clamp around another man's neck.

His gaze swept the chamber, but he found it empty save her.

They were very much alone.

"I am thinking about the grave error I made in opening my gates to you on the basis of Christian charity." Her cold words were underscored by her stiff carriage. Tension threaded through her voice, hinting at a wealth of emotion beneath the hauteur.

Only, the scent of her remained as inviting as always.

Just now, he found it difficult to believe he could melt that icy exterior.

"Why choose this chamber for errant thoughts that will not change the past?" He gestured to the vacant pallet. "Is this where you meet your lover? Do you confide your regrets in the father of your child, perhaps?"

"You are an ill-mannered lout to suggest it, but I am not surprised your thoughts are so base." She lifted the hem of her surcoat and swept around to one arrow slit that overlooked the courtyard. The opening had been covered with some kind of thin skin that muted the view but allowed light to show through.

Weak winter sun touched her hair, bathing her outline in warm color. Seeing her thus reminded him of fanciful thoughts he'd once had about her. There had been a time when he seemed to light up inside just looking upon her. Not just because of her beauty but because of her nurturing spirit. The ease with which she looked after her clan.

Though she'd been the younger sister, she'd always seemed so responsible. Practical.

How foolish he'd been.

"Then why are you here? I have scoured the keep and seen no sign of you for hours. It will be easy enough to discover who last occupied this chamber. The maids will not be so loyal to you when you are no longer their mistress. They will answer me when I ask."

Jealousy made him crueler than necessary, he knew. But her secretive nature ever since he'd returned to Domhnaill spurred his suspicions.

"There is no need to ask the maids my business. I can tell you that I sought Lord Cullen of Blackstone this afternoon to accept a proposal of marriage he once suggested to my father."

If he'd been an impassive bystander, he might have admired her shrewd political acumen in such a move that could easily unseat Duncan and his claim to the keep. He needed Domhnaill to secure Culcanon and settle the rift with Donegal.

But he'd never been impassive when it came to this woman.

"Your father will not permit such a match." Duncan closed the distance between them, tempted to seize her by the shoulders and shake sense back into her. "And if he does agree to it, it will be easy enough for me to prove to the king that he is no longer sound in his thinking."

His hands clenched and unclenched at his sides, powerless in anger toward a woman.

"You would not."

"Do not tempt me."

She remained silent for a long moment, fury simmering in her gray eyes.

"Well?" he prodded, his anger restless and in need of a target. He did not care if it was Blackstone, the laird of Domhnaill or the king himself. "What was Blackstone's response? Did you at least warn the man whose wrath he would incur if he accepted you?"

"Apparently a matter of some urgency called him home unexpectedly. I was not able to speak with him."

Relief flooded through him. The crushing weight that had been on his chest dissipated into nothing. He wanted to laugh with the unexpected good news, but the dark cloud of her expression made him reconsider.

But, saints be praised, he'd won a reprieve.

"Do not look so disappointed, lass." He tipped up her chin, unwilling to think she found him so abhorrent that wedding a man more than twice her age would be preferable. "Whether you know it or not, Cullen's absence has saved innocent lives. I will not have to fight him for you now."

"My hand is still mine to give," she protested, turning away.

He missed the feel of her skin against his fingers.

That brief contact had calmed him and stirred him at the same time.

"As a noblewoman?" He shook his head. "I think not. If your father does not will a marriage with Blackstone, what choices do you have? It is one thing to refuse marriage altogether, but no woman of your standing is allowed to choose her own mate. There is too much at stake."

"And you think I do not appreciate that? I, who have worked to develop a thriving trade here out of nothing? I, who have added to Domhnaill's coffers far more than I have taken? Yet now, I must step aside and watch my hard work go to ruin in the hands of a warrior who lives by the sword and not by the land?"

She stalked about the dim chamber, as restless in her outrage as he'd been with his own. He had not expected her to protest his rule on these grounds. Nor had he realized how much she'd grown to enjoy her mead-making.

Enjoy her. His onetime enemy.

He had to keep her here. After the way he'd tricked her, he could not allow her to lose her position. Not after all the time he'd spent with her. He'd seen what an effective lady she made to her people.

"What makes you think Blackstone would have been any different? He is a warrior, too, although an older one. But I told you once before that you would have a place here if I took over as laird."

"As the mistress of mead, not as a wife with any

power." She shook her head impatiently. "Do you think I can go from being lady here to servant, no matter how lucrative?"

She vastly exaggerated the change in position, but he understood her point. Following her back to the window casement, where she stared moodily out the filmy covering, he placed his hands on her shoulders and spun her to face him.

He could only see one option. He did not know if that's because he wanted her or because he'd entered her keep by treachery that first time. Either way, he needed to end all talk of Blackstone.

"Then do not be a servant under the new rule. Speak the vows to me you should have said years ago and be my wife."

Chapter Seven

Cristiana did not know what made her heart thump so fiercely.

Was it the fear of a proposal that could cost her a future with Leah? Tender surprise at Duncan's willingness to wed her even though he thought her innocence had been stolen by another man?

Or was it simply the feel of his strong, warm hands upon her person, exciting her the way his touch always had? Either way, her racing heart confused her. She felt unsteady and unsure of herself in the wake of an emotional day.

"What purpose will such an arrangement serve for you?" she found herself asking, though she should have simply denied the request.

"You are well-loved by your people. Wedding you will help them accept me."

It was true. Yet believing him meant she had to recognize he cared about such things. That a well-meaning heart lurked beneath his arrogance and maneuvering.

"The people would grow to respect you either way." Her eyes sought his, the green darker than her daughter's but sharing a distinct pattern of yellow flecks throughout.

She noticed he had not removed his hands from shoulders, the fingers beginning a subtle stroke inward toward her neck.

"Aye. But I have need of a wife and I found you admirably suited the first time I looked into the matter." A light, teasing tone crept into his words, tempting her to relax into the moment. "Besides, I have great need of fat coffers. Apparently you can deliver them to me through this mead-making prowess of yours."

Of course she could not marry him. But that gentle tone of his—as if they shared secrets and confidences—tried telling her differently.

"Much has changed in five years," she reminded him, hoping she could dissuade him from his course. She feared the wandering direction of his hands even more than the conspiratorial whispers. "I am not so well suited anymore."

If that did not deter him from this union, she was lost. Her father and Keane already demanded it. If Duncan wished it in spite of her supposed lack of innocence, she would be wed to him whether she willed it or nay.

"We have all changed." His thumbs strayed over her collarbone to the neck of her linen kirtle. "You have turned into a woman of great talent and ambition. You've used it to further your family's fame and wealth. I admire that, since my half brother increased our rents in my absence and used all the gain to indulge his temper with ill-chosen border wars."

She stilled, captive to his touch and surprised at the sudden dark undertone to his words. Had she misjudged his relationship with Donegal? Could Duncan have seen the ugly side of his half brother's character even though he had often defended him publicly?

"I think it is right to put family before all else," she admitted, breathing in the clean scent of his skin underneath the hint of hickory smoke that clung to his garb from some hearth fire.

She really needed to extricate herself from the vacant chamber where they were far too alone. But just now, she couldn't even seem to untwine herself from his sweetly seductive hands as he squeezed her closer.

"You see? We are one in this thinking. We are both ready to protect and defend those closest to us." His gaze drew her in until she got lost in it. Spellbound by the connection, she did not sense the impending kiss until his lips brushed her cheek.

Her temple.

Swaying on her feet, she blinked and tried to reorient herself. Blindly, she gripped his tunic, steadying herself.

Perhaps he would understand her need to protect Leah, no matter what. Perhaps he would fall in love with the little girl as much as she had. But she could not count on it. She must demand it ere she went any further.

"Wait." She edged back, knowing she could not go forward unless she ensured Leah's safety. "I cannot—I will not—allow this unless you can assure me you will protect Leah."

He frowned. Shook his head.

"Of course." He leaned in to kiss her, his breath warm upon her neck. "Whatever you wish."

"Nay." She held him off, trembling within. "It is not enough. You must…" she said as she licked her lips. "You must swear it to me."

He straightened fully, though he did not release her. Confusion and a fair amount of righteous indignation passed through his gaze.

"She is at risk somehow?" He studied her more carefully. "You have reason to believe she is in danger."

"Nay. But as long as her father draws breath, I will worry that he might come back for her. This, I will not tolerate."

Perhaps it was the mention of the child's father. But something in her words caused a tightening of his jaw. An angry flare of the nostrils. But this time he did not hesitate to give her what she wished.

"By all I hold holy, I swear to you, I will keep Leah with my own life."

Transfixed by the fierceness of the oath, she was silent a long moment.

"You would prefer I draw blood to seal the matter?" he asked, without a trace of hesitation.

"Nay." She nodded jerkily, overwhelmed at the security she had just claimed for her child. Without question, she had obtained a stalwart protector for Leah. She just prayed Duncan would not come to despise her for all the secrets she kept. "The oath— your words—they are sufficient."

"Then come to me," he whispered, pulling her closer. "My service comes with a price and I plan to collect it tonight."

His lips brushed her cheek. The tenderness of that touch, combined with a binding vow that she had not expected, softened her last shred of resistance. Maybe the time had come to seize the moment of happiness that had been teasing her senses every time she'd ever been in Duncan's presence.

"I have lingered with you too long." The soft words were not a chastisement so much as an admission of fact. She couldn't have walked out now if she'd tried.

He squeezed her to him, his hands skimming up

her spine. Her breasts molded to his chest, her legs brushed his thighs.

"Nay. You have not lingered nearly long enough." His errant hand that had toyed with her neckline earlier now thrust deeply beneath the fabric, trailing along the swell of her breast. Heat bubbled along her skin. Like a cauldron nearing the boiling point, the warmth concentrated on the outside first, but she knew it was only a matter of time before that fire reached the inside.

Still, with her last grip on rational thought, she arched up on her toes to better gaze into his eyes.

"You've not won fairly," she accused.

"Since we are hardly fighting, I will consider it a victory for us both."

His mouth covered hers, quieting all worries and any extraneous thought. There was only this moment. Him.

Her whole body turned liquid and boneless at the stroke of his tongue. Lights danced behind her closed eyes as he surrounded her. Absorbed her into him. She wrapped her arms about his neck, needing to get closer to the source of all that vibrant feeling animating her limbs. Her belly. Her most secret places.

She recalled this sinful feeling from other kisses. Other times she'd been alone with him. But the intoxication in her blood was stronger now than ever, perhaps because she knew she would see it through this time. This kiss would not end until she had explored that feeling and savored it for herself. She knew Duncan could provide it in full measure—a night of heaven on earth.

With tingling fingers, she splayed her hands along his broad shoulders, spanning thick muscle and flesh-warmed linen. If her blind groping was too brazen, she did not care. Men knew the source of all this hot frenzy, but she did not. Fumbling with the ties of his tunic, she freed the laces until the shirt loosened enough to make way for her touch.

"I have dreamed of you," he confessed, breaking off the kiss long enough to tug the tunic up and off. "Dreamed of this."

Taking his hand, she led him toward the pallet and the room's only source of light—the narrow window casement with the tapestry pulled to one side.

"It is not enough to see each other in dreams. I want to remember exactly how you look." She eyed him hungrily, taking in the bands of muscle that started beneath his ribs and disappeared into his braies.

"Wait here," he warned her, stepping away from her when she'd been ready to leap back into his arms. "I would like to see you better, as well."

Confused, she watched him hasten from the room, bare chested and magnificent. He returned in a trice with a torch in hand. Shoving the door closed behind him, he lowered the bar to seal them in privacy and then approached the hearth. He tossed the torch into the grate atop a small pile of wood, casting the small

chamber in a golden glow. Cristiana watched the way
the fire bathed his body in burnished bronze, admir-
ing the sleek perfection of his honed strength.

He studied her, too. His dark green gaze caressed
her, lingering on her bare shoulder, where her kirtle
had slipped down. Self-consciously, her hand went
there, brushing her bare skin with her fingers as if
he'd bid her to do so. As if she could not wait another
moment to feel a true caress.

"Duncan." She called to him, his name a hoarse
plea when her body already trembled for him.

"Take it off," he bid her, his own voice gruff with
hunger. "I will fix the pallet so it is fit to lay you there.
But I would like to see—"

Fingers flying over the laces, she unfastened the
surcoat and let it slide to the floor.

He'd been freeing a tapestry from the wall—pre-
sumably to lay upon the pallet. He tore it down with
gratifying speed at the sight of her in the thin lawn
kirtle.

She guessed the hearth fire illuminated her body
from behind. The flames felt good against her back
when she'd started undressing. She did not need to
look down to know her breasts fit snug inside the
garment. The soft fabric—normally so comfortable—
chafed her overly sensitive skin. She wanted his hands
upon her and nothing more.

"You are—" he seemed to search for words, his
eyes never leaving her body as he tossed the tapestry

unceremoniously upon the straw-filled mattress "—a feast for the eyes."

She shifted her weight from one foot to the other, eager for his touch.

"Then I hope you've brought an appetite," she teased, lifting her hands to her hair to untwine the plaits. "It will be my pleasure to serve you."

She was on her back in a flash.

A primal thrill shot through her at the sweet feminine joy of being overpowered. The weight of him squeezed and tantalized her even as he propped himself on an elbow to bear some of the burden. She had not guessed she could have such a strong effect on him, to lure him so thoroughly to bed.

Her half-undone hair fell about her shoulders, a silken coverlet between her and the tapestry beneath her. He buried his nose in the untwining curls, breathing in her scent.

"You smell like honey. I cannot drink mead without thinking of you." He gripped the hem of her kirtle where it drifted about her thighs and skimmed it up her legs.

Baring her hips.

Her breath caught in her throat as her heartbeat raced.

"I will spoil your taste for all others," she warned, savoring the feel of his hand at her waist. Skin on skin at last.

She gave herself to him so wholly, so eagerly,

perhaps he would never realize she was so innocent. Heaven knew she wanted him with the fevered urgency of a female in heat.

"You did that long ago." He cupped her bottom in his palm, startling a gasp from her as he guided her hips toward his staff. Even through his braies, she could feel the length and thickness of him.

A shiver of delight mingled with fear. Mayhap he would recognize maidenly resistance all too well.

"Have mercy, my lord," she murmured, her words tumbling out too fast while she tried to catch her breath. "You will be my undoing."

"Count on it," he vowed, spreading her thighs with his. "It's my turn to spoil your taste for all others now."

With his teeth, he nipped the neck of her kirtle and raked it down, exposing her breasts. He plucked at one tight peak between his thumb and forefinger, eliciting a cry of sharp yearning. Desire flowed thick and fast in her veins. Slick, feminine heat drenched the tender, sensitive place between her thighs. He must have felt that warm wanting.

Idly, she raked her nails over his hips, tugging ineffectually at his braies. She wanted what came next—even if it meant her last secret was revealed. She had a woman's right to know true pleasure with a man who understood how to provide it.

"Take me," she whispered, thrashing this way and

that on the pallet underneath the sweet torment of his thumb circling her nipple.

In answer, he licked the swollen crest and nipped it between his teeth. Her hips bucked in response, as if an invisible cord connected that place where he licked and sucked with the throbbing spot between her legs. The physical joy of it was merciless.

At last, one hand dipped down her belly to sift through the damp curls shielding her sex. She made soft, crooning noises in her throat that she could not possibly stifle. The feel of his fingers sliding along the slick folds was enough to drive her to madness.

Still, he took his time, his tongue working over the peak of her breast with the same thorough attention as his finger massaged that sweet spot between her thighs.

In the dark recesses of her brain, she recognized the movement of his free hand along the ties of his braies, freeing his sex. She could feel the heat of his shaft along her thigh. But mostly, she could only pay attention to the anticipation coiling tight in her womb. Her fingers threaded through his dark hair, holding his mouth to her breast while his thumb worked the tight bud hidden at her core. Just when she thought she could take no more, just when the fire had built to unbearable temperatures, something within her seemed to snap.

Waves of pleasure clenched her insides, squeezing her over and over again. She cried out in sweet surprise, not having realized a man could do such decadently wonderful things to a woman.

It was while her heart thundered through the bliss that he positioned himself between her legs. She felt the thick heat of him there, stretching the entrance of her womanly passage.

Tensing, she gripped his shoulders. That trickle of fear came back, but it was smaller now with the overwhelming gratification still coursing through her. She whispered his name. Trusting him. Putting herself in his hands.

She gazed up at him in the firelight and saw the set to his jaw. The sheen of sweat on his skin. He'd been holding back for her. Giving her a taste of passion before this—joining. She could see that now.

But the time for holding back was done and she could feel it in the way he eased inside her. Growled deep in his throat. Withdrew his hips.

Bracing herself, she readied for what was to come and still the sting of it scared a cry from her lips. Something inside her tore. Her maidenhead, she knew. She'd hoped it would be a smaller thing. A negligible thing he might not notice at all.

Yet the brief furrow of his eyebrows, the confusion and perhaps anger she saw in his eyes, told her that he very much noticed. Ducking her head into his shoulder, she held on to him and waited for the pain to subside.

Thankfully, he did not take that moment to berate

her. He seemed as bound up in hunger as she'd been earlier. He needed to find the bliss that she'd already experienced.

She tried to find that sweet rhythm again but though the soreness had dulled the ache between her legs had not totally dissipated. Mostly, she held on tight to him, praying she would find forgiveness with him later. That he would understand.

When he found his release, she felt the powerful surge of his body. On some level, she savored the connection even as she feared the aftermath. Right now, he was a part of her and she of him. And she could see in the glazed expression of his eyes that he had been as transformed—however briefly—as she'd been. Why else would he hold her so tenderly afterward, as their hearts beat in like rhythm?

Still, she was not prepared for the fierceness in his voice when he rolled to her side and pulled her along with him.

"You are mine now." His green eyes glittered dangerously as he gripped her chin and forced her gaze to his. "There will be no more lies between us."

She bristled, unprepared for confrontation while her emotions were as tender and exposed as the rest of her.

"You are no stranger to deceit," she reminded him, scrambling to find some defense.

She would gladly start an argument to divert him. Yet he did not appear to be a man who would be easily dissuaded from his course. And truth be told, what they had shared had weakened her. Softened her.

Heaven help her.

"You will not leave this bed until you tell me the truth," he warned, his heavy leg coming to rest between her thighs in subtle reminder of his strength. "Why have you claimed your sister's child as your own?"

Chapter Eight

"Leah is an orphan. I have taken her in to keep her safe."

Duncan searched for the truth in Cristiana's eyes as he lay over her, his blood still pounding from the eye-crossing release he'd found in taking her. Part of him was furious about this newest lie uncovered. But another part of him was still pumping a victorious fist in the air that he had been the first to claim her. The first to breach her tender walls.

She had not lain with some random man. She'd merely taken in a child to raise. A child she cared about enough to impart her name and shed her honor. A child who bore her distinct resemblance. It could only be the daughter of her exiled sister.

"Do not mince words," he warned, berating himself for letting her chase him off so easily five years ago.

Perhaps if he had demanded she honor their contract then, there might have been tenderness between them instead of lies and regret. "The girl is of your blood. Since I now know she is not your daughter, she can belong only to Edwina."

Cristiana remained mutinously silent, but he could see the pulse throb nervously in her neck. She did not want to admit the truth that was so plain.

"Why will you not confess it? You can't honestly believe you are fooling anyone under your own roof—" But then the truth hit him. Or at least some portion of it. "Your father lost his wife when this child would have been born. And his health has failed enough that he cannot run his own keep. Could it be you have kept the truth of a grandchild from him?"

"Have you considered all the children my randy grandfather is rumored to have begotten? Just look around the village and you will see half a dozen people who bear close resemblance to my family!"

He knew she was only trying to throw him off the scent, yet the story could have been true.

"She is mine." Cristiana drew out the short statement, emphasizing every word as if he were as shaky on wits as her sire. "You have never believed anything I've said unless it confirms your own beliefs, however. Now, I demand you let me go."

He was so taken aback by her ridiculous accusation that he did release her. While she smoothed her kirtle and retrieved her surcoat, he allowed her words to roll about his brain. Was he too quick to believe the worst of her? He had certainly accepted her assertion that she was no maid.

"You are still angry that I did not believe you when you claimed Donegal ravaged Edwina against her will."

"I have made that clear more than once." She struggled into her sleeves and fumbled with a golden girdle that encircled her hips. "You did not trust me then. And I am not sure how much I can trust you now, although I will hold you to the vow you made to me about Leah."

"I could not call myself a knight if I did not maintain such a pledge."

She nodded shortly. Clearly, she would trust him with that and little else. But then, she was still stinging from his maneuvering his way into her keep and into a marriage she did not want.

But one day, he would win her. For now, he only wanted to discover the truth of Leah's parentage.

"So you kept Edwina's secret all this time," he mused, hoping she would admit what he'd already guessed.

Sighing, Cristina shrugged.

"What else could I do? Donegal brutalized her, and she was too ashamed to show herself to anyone who could confirm scratches and bruises left on private places. She swore me to silence to keep what peace we could between our families, but she could not find the heart to embrace a child made in so much pain."

Her sharp words finally found their mark. The evidence that had been there all along now berated him for his own blindness. Donegal was more monstrous than he knew. Treachery to family was a sin, but Duncan had excused it to a degree because Donegal had been raised by a serving wench instead of at his side as was his right. Duncan had tried to atone for that lack in Donegal's childhood, but in his guilt he must have missed the signs of his half brother's dark side.

Abusing a woman was such a base crime. It was not a simple sin of greed, but a dark violence that demonstrated a complete lack of honor.

"You have done a noble thing to take in an unwanted child." He knew from Donegal's experience that an illegitimate babe could suffer the sins of the parents. "I am sorry I did not believe you when you first told me that Edwina suffered at Donegal's hands."

Cristiana's busy hands stilled, the laces of her surcoat drooping at her sides. Her mouth opened and then closed, as if she could not find the response she wanted. Finally, she gave a curt nod.

"Thank you."

"But now we must correct the mistakes of the past and claim the child as our own when we announce our marriage." He peered toward the skin covering the window and noted the sun had gone down completely.

They were both late to sup with their guests before they departed on the morrow. "We cannot allow the girl to be raised in back corridors with serving maids and minstrels for companions. She needs the security of knowing her place in the world."

"You will claim to be her father?" She folded her arms and squeezed them tightly to her while she worried her lower lip with her teeth.

"Of course. She will bear me as much resemblance as you." He arose to begin dressing. Much work remained to be done to ensure a smooth transfer of power.

"You will not let Donegal take her?" The dark fear in her eyes could not have been more plain. This, at last, was the real reason she hid the child from the world.

Ah, how much hurt might have been avoided if they could have trusted each other long ago?

"Never." He would need to deal with his brother at some point, but he could promise this much to ease Cristiana's fears. "But we must announce our marriage and claim her as our own tonight."

Her shoulders sagged with relief.

"Leah is my only concern." Her fingers returned to her surcoat laces as she tied the garment into place. "As long as she is safe and she is with me, I will agree to most anything."

As he finished dressing, he felt a hollowness in his chest. Her response was hardly a passionate avowal.

But perhaps they had missed their chance for a union of abiding trust and friendship. How strange that he would finally claim Cristiana as his own, yet he felt none of the happy expectation that had awaited them on their first betrothal.

Now, they were united in a common cause to protect a child that was not theirs. And a passion that she'd succumbed to only because she could not locate an aging lord to wed instead.

"May I escort you to sup?" he asked, extending an arm to her when he really wished to return to their pallet and seek the heated connection they'd shared so recently.

Somehow, they'd remained cool strangers despite everything.

"Of course," she murmured, distracted and still nibbling the fullness of her lower lip.

Her thoughts were elsewhere. And it occurred to him that although he'd secured her hand and forced the marriage he'd needed, he hadn't really won her— Cristiana, the woman—at all.

She had betrayed her sister.

Cristiana had no choice, of course. But would Edwina see it that way when she learned a Culcanon would rule Domhnaill and claim Leah after all? She brushed the feathered end of her quill along her cheek, savoring the soft touch, as she oversaw the move of Leah's few possessions into Cristiana's chamber.

Once again, she attempted a letter to her sister. Once again, the right words were difficult to come by. Duncan had said she should invite her sister to return home and he would try to find an appropriate match for her—one that would further all their fortunes, yet give Edwina to a husband who would be both grateful for her and understanding of her lack of innocence.

But how could she convey that on a cold and unforgiving piece of parchment?

"Mother, look at the flames!" Leah stood before the hearth fire with a handful of herbs. As she tossed them into the fire, the flames turned colors and smoked merrily. A gift from the cook, no doubt, who always seemed to have some new diversion for the girl.

"How pretty," Cristiana exclaimed, grateful that Leah had grown intrigued with the fire instead of the thousand and one questions she seemed to have about her new change in status.

After Duncan's announcement at sup two days ago, the whole keep had been unsettled at the news that Leah was Cristiana and Duncan's biological daughter. Some people had not believed it at all, suspecting the story had been concocted as a cover to give a name to a little girl with whom Cristiana was besotted. But most were only too glad for the lurid gossip that ensued.

And truly, what should people believe? She should be happy that Duncan had vowed to protect Leah from his half brother. She'd said all along that would be enough for her. But as she sat before the hearth, facing an awkward letter to her sister, more awkward explanations to Leah and a marriage that had only come about through lies and deception, Cristiana could not help a twinge of regret.

"Crissie?" A knock at the door accompanied the voice outside her solar.

The servants arranging Leah's trunk in the bed-chamber hurried out to open the solar door for the old laird.

Her father stood in the doorway with a deeply fur-rowed expression, his robes askew as if he'd escaped from his chamber before being properly groomed for the day. At a glance, she could see he was confused. Anxious.

She set down her parchment and quill to rise and greet him.

"Father." She reached out to him, but Leah beat her to the older man's side. The child threw herself against his legs and squeezed.

"Grandfather!" Leah had always been close to the laird. Adopting the familial endearment with Cristi-ana's father the same way she had for Cristiana. But then, neither of them discouraged the practice as they were a family by practice if not by blood ties. The old laird had taken an interest in the new baby in the keep as a welcome distraction in the wake of his wife's death.

Domhnaill had raised more than one orphan, so the acceptance of the green-eyed girl had not been all that unusual in the keep.

Still, he did not look pleased today. He patted the girl's head absently and then steered her back toward the hearth, all the while glaring darkly at his daughter.

"You lied to me." His voice cracked with an anger she'd never seen directed toward her before. "I sent your sister away because of you."

"Mother?" Leah looked over at them, worried.

Cristiana gestured to the maids to take the child and leave them.

"I will come for you soon, sweeting, and we will move your favorite tapestry above the bed," she assured the child on her way out. "But let me speak to your grandfather first."

"I thought her spoiled for marriage," her father railed, raising his voice. "Yet it was you who was not fit to wed. *You* who said you would not marry because you did not fancy any man."

His accusations speared her heart all the more for knowing she would never be able to untangle the lies from the truth in his mind. Even if he understood the truth today, he would just as easily forget it by the morrow.

"Father, Edwina will come home." She pointed to the half-filled parchment. "I am writing to her now, so she will return to us."

"But you have robbed me of her for four long years! My own girl. Your mother would never have allowed it." He ranted and grumbled, paced and prowled about the floor, his robe sliding from his diminished shoulders now and again so that she had to chase him to replace it and risk a snarling rebuke.

By the time Keane arrived at the door, perhaps notified by the maids who'd taken Leah from the chamber, Cristiana's eyes stung with tears.

"Ach, lass, you know better than to listen to him when he does not know his own words," Keane admonished, barging in without knocking and without preamble. Bandy-legged and stooped but sound in mind at least, he steered the laird toward the door with a strength that belied his years. "Do you hear me, girl? He loves you, dear. It would hurt him sorely to know he wounded you, but he does not know what he speaks of."

Cristiana nodded mutely, grateful for the reassurance even though she knew her father's accusations would linger. She had woven a tangled web, no doubt, even if her father did not quite have the right of it.

"Thank you for retrieving him." She opened the door to ease their way out. "I hope he will be well enough to attend the nuptials."

In spite of Duncan's vow to Leah, there had been no suggestion of tender feeling between them and no indication that their future would be tempered by the softer sentiments they'd once shared. How would she bear the day without at least one family member to stand beside her?

Keane shook his head.

"Not unless you want to risk accusations before the priest. He has ranted for days since he found out the girl is your daughter. I do not think he will come around until some new event claims his fractured attention."

Cristiana found herself nodding her understanding even though she didn't understand at all. Why couldn't Keane explain the truth to the old laird on the wedding day, just to get him through the ceremony quietly?

Perhaps because Keane believed that she had betrayed them all—and Edwina most especially—as well.

"Of course." On impulse, she leaned to kiss her father's cheek despite his growling protest and an unkind word. "I am sorry, my lord."

The two of them exited the chamber, leaving her more alone than she'd ever been since Edwina had departed. At least in those early days she'd had the company of a squalling, red-faced infant who had needed her for everything. Now, she'd lost her father's respect and affection. She felt needed for very little here, other than to legitimize Duncan's claim to a keep he'd been planning to take one way or another from the moment he'd set foot over her gate.

Steeling herself for her sister's reaction to the

news of her wedding, Cristiana settled in to finish the letter to Edwina. No matter what the elder Domhnaill daughter thought of the nuptials, she was needed at home immediately. Her exile was over at last.

Edwina dreamed of Cullen.

The sweet innocence of her nighttime interlude with him—a fanciful garden flirtation that came from the heart and not from cold machinations—made it so much harder to rise from her bed to accomplish the task she'd set for herself this night. Curse her naive imaginings.

But she had no choice. She'd just received a letter her sister posted a sennight ago. A Culcanon as laird? Over her dead body.

Dressing in a softly worn surcoat that she strategically laced only partway, Edwina rubbed her hands together to warm them in the cold chamber she shared with three other ladies-in-waiting to their stern Norman mistress. Edwina had only been in this household since the previous spring, but she'd always travelled to points north with the court when William and his knights moved about. She'd stayed on in Evesburh, purposely proving extremely helpful to the lady who ran the keep that had last hosted the court.

As Edwina loosened her plaited hair and pinched her nipples to make them stand stiff beneath her thin garb, she reminded herself how well she'd planned her little interlude tonight.

Henry had guard duty and would be alone in the tower for another three hours. She'd ensured her chamber mates had drank their fill of good mead at mealtime, purposely choosing this night to educate the table on the finer points of mead-making that she recalled from Cristiana.

The memory of her sister was yet another chink in her armor as she swept out of her chamber and rushed toward the west tower. Like her dream of Cullen, Cristiana was a spot of kindness in her past that she sometimes feared she was dishonoring through her behavior. Would Cristiana tease a good man with sexual favors to obtain revenge on another? Of course not. Cristiana was a mother now. A good, kind mother who would raise Leah the way Edwina's sweet baby deserved.

Her eyes burned at the thought while she climbed the drafty, narrow stairs toward the guard tower. But Cristiana had not been defiled by a brute, and so she could not know what decisions Edwina had been faced with since leaving Domhnaill. There were some choices no woman should have to make.

Lifting her chin, she steeled her heart and flung open the guard-tower door, ready for the biggest performance of her life. Perhaps she could find a good woman for Henry when they got to Scotland. But for tonight, Edwina needed his strength and his sword arm, his stalwart honor and his absolute, undivided sexual attention.

"Edwina." He turned from his spot overlooking the drawbridge when she opened the door, his longbow quickly falling to his side.

Only then, seeing the arrow dipped toward the stone floor, did it occur to her that he might have shot an intruder in the dark. A small swell of panic mingled with relief and fueled the worry in her voice.

"Henry." She breathed hard, all the better to press her breasts tight to her surcoat. She did not need the small torch burning on one wall to know his gaze dropped to the outline of stiff, swollen nipples visible through her worn linen surcoat and thinnest kirtle. "I cannot sleep. I'm so distraught."

He swallowed visibly. Gulped, actually. Her heart turned over in her chest. But had Donegal the Wretched felt any sympathy toward her when she'd been scared and crying? Nay. She could not relent now.

"What's wrong?" Henry's voice was deep and masculine. If she'd not just had such a fond dream of Cullen, she might have been tempted to simply give Henry everything he wanted of her.

"I have been too demanding of you when I should be so grateful for your generous offer. You have treated me so kindly and so honorably when my reputation does not warrant such kindness—"

"Don't say that." He dropped the longbow on the rampart and took a step closer, but he did not touch her. "You have not been demanding. Every woman is entitled to have her family around her when she weds."

She shook her head, her half-plaited hair slipping loose even more. She'd visited the baths the day before, scrubbing her body with rose water and her hair with a pilfered bit of scented soap from her lady's storeroom. Edwina knew she smelled like a floral field in springtime. Her partially laced surcoat slipped a bit down her shoulders with the motion, the heavier fabric tugging at her kirtle and bearing just a hint of her collarbone.

"No. I am an outcast and I have no reason to think they've forgiven me for my sins." She had not been clear with Henry about her past, although everyone knew she'd been a selective courtesan in the king's court and a ruined woman from the moment she'd arrived. Still, he must wonder a little at the reputation, when she'd been with no man since arriving in Evesburh. Mostly, that was because the Norman woman ran a very moral household. But also because Edwina had been exceedingly careful not to stray anywhere alone with a man.

Save Henry. She'd seen his goodness immediately.

"You must not talk like that." He did touch her now, his strong arm going about her waist before she dissolved in a heap of tears at his feet. "I see the sweetness in you. Whatever life has forced upon you, I know it was not deserved. You are a good woman."

Her distraught state gave her an excuse to lean

heavily into him, her breasts pressed tight to his broad chest. But oh, his kind words tested her all over again. His staff was as rigid as a dagger against her belly, the weapon a formidable one. Lightly, she lay a hand upon his hip and swore she would find him the most pure and innocent virgin in all the Highlands as his reward for taking her home.

Predictably, his sword lengthened and strained closer at her soft touch so near.

"And you are the kindest man." Were truer words ever spoken? "That is why I cannot see you any longer. No more long looks after sup. No stolen dances when the minstrels play. I am going to return to court and forget we ever met."

He cursed. He pleaded. And finally, before his shift was over, he agreed to take her home to be with her family when they wed. Edwina took no pride in a performance that would lead to heartbreak for Henry. But she had won the battle with the only weapons she'd known these past four years.

She was going home to Domhnaill.

And by the saints, she would wreak her vengeance on the Culcanons. First for Donegal the Worm's brutal deflowering. Then for the disbelieving naysaying from Duncan and their father. Cristiana might have trouble keeping the Culcanon traitors out of their home, but Edwina would use any means necessary to ensure the Culcanons rued the day they crossed her.

* * *

Duncan had won.

The keep. The woman. The resources to secure Culcanon in the wake of his brother's draining reign.

Yet the victory felt more hollow than any in memory. It was this hollowness that had brought him into the Domhnaill chapel to pray late one night after his men had bedded down in the great hall for the eve. The guilt of such a victory had brought him to his knees in front of a dour-looking saint that watched over the nave with grave eyes.

Candles flickered at the statue's feet, the flames blowing hard to the west thanks to the draft edging in below the main doors. Duncan searched for the right words to find forgiveness for the way he'd muscled Cristiana into marriage.

Nay, he wanted forgiveness for seducing an innocent before her wedding day. He would not have resorted to such tactics if he'd realized she was untouched. Indeed, she would never have given herself to him so readily if she had not thought she was out of options. By allowing her to think he'd obtained the full backing of their king for his bid to take Domhnaill, he had pushed too hard for his own ends.

Therefore, he took comfort in the aching of his knees as he bartered with the unmoving saint in the chapel nave. As long as he proved a strong mate to Cristiana, he need not feel the sting of guilt.

And this he would do.

Somehow, he would soften her toward him before she discovered all the ways he'd taken advantage of her father's weakened rule. His terms meted out with the saint, Duncan rose to his feet and crossed himself before leaving the nave.

It was fortunate that his prayers were so much on his mind as he left the chapel and returned to the main keep. Otherwise, he might not have been able to tamp down the surge of anger that came from spying Cristiana hurrying through the darkened hall, clinging to Rory the Lothian's side.

Hadn't Rory offered for her himself? Clearly he coveted Duncan's future bride. That much would have been apparent simply from the way he inclined his head toward her to hear her speak. The knight's arm was wrapped protectively—possessively?—about her as they sneaked quietly around the sleeping figures in the great hall.

Did they slip away to be together?

"Remove your hands from her." Duncan's voice would have awoken half the hall if most of the inhabitants hadn't been drunk, as well as sleeping.

Rory and Cristiana stilled together.

Frozen by guilt?

But then Cristiana launched through the dark shapes prone on the floor, hurrying toward him with her skirts in one hand and what appeared to be a rolled parchment in the other.

"We have been searching for you," she whispered, her eyes wide. "A messenger arrived from the king. He would not rest until he gave you this, but he appeared half dead from a hard ride and I insisted he eat and rest while I found you."

She thrust the parchment under his nose, her hair in pleasing disarray. Because she'd risen from her bed to see a messenger? He knew that must be the case, but he could not rid the memory of Rory's arm about her. What tenderness lay between them?

Duncan took the message and pulled her close, heedless of decorum.

"I will read it and speak with him immediately. Await me in your solar and I will be there shortly."

He needed to talk to her about whatever the message contained, of course, and he wanted to warn her about Rory's feelings for her. Perhaps he also wanted an opportunity to reassure himself that she did not return those feelings.

But as soon as he'd spoken, he realized how the command sounded. As if they already shared a bedchamber.

True, not many were awake enough to have heard the exchange. But he had not lowered his voice, and the news of it would still fill the keep by the morrow.

Her cheeks burned hot, the pink flush of color obvious even by the flickering light of a hearth fire across the hall.

"As you wish," she told him shortly, glaring daggers at him as she attempted to disentangle herself from his arm.

Reluctantly he freed her, knowing he needed to give his undivided attention to the missive. After she stormed away, he broke the seal on the parchment and neared the great hall fire, the only blaze casting enough light by which to read.

"You do her injustice to mistrust her." Rory's voice followed him, taunting him with what he already knew.

He turned on his friend, fists tightening at his sides.

"And you do me injury to touch my betrothed."

"By the saints, Duncan. She's seen what a man's temper can do to a woman. Do you really think it wise to fling your temper around like a caged bear when she has only just barely agreed to wed?"

Belatedly, he realized he'd crumpled a royal missive in his clenched hand. Curse the Lothian for being such a voice of reason. The memory of Cristiana's crestfallen expression bit his conscience.

"Is it wise for you to put a hand on a woman I lost once already?"

Until he spoke the words, he had not fully appreciated how much the loss of Cristiana had hurt the first time. He'd told himself back then that there were many other smart, sensual women that would make good wives. But in truth, he'd wanted no one but Cristiana.

"If you cannot trust your second in command to protect those you care for, *who* will you put your faith in?" Rory did not await an answer, turning on his boot heel and stalking out.

With a frustrated snarl, Duncan kicked an oversized log into the flames. The scent of hickory and pine wafted up from the hearth, sending sparks showering over the leg of his braies. Nearby, a sleeping old woman snorted and turned away from the rising blaze.

Shoving aside his mistakes with Cristiana, he unfurled the parchment and read:

Your brother's men have attacked mine under your banner. If you cannot put down the rebel factions in your clan, I will march on Culcanon in three days' time.

Three days.

He had not even planned his nuptials for another sennight. How would he secure Domhnaill, his bride and Culcanon in that time? Had his time abroad in battle and diplomacy bought him so little from Malcolm?

Once again, he would pay for his brother's sins.

Casting the missive into the flames with an oath, he watched it blaze into nothingness. He had not come so far to lose everything. With or without the bonds of marriage, he would leave Domhnaill at once with Cristiana at his side.

Chapter Nine

"This is madness." Cristiana's hoarse whisper was lost in the frenzy of sleepy-eyed servants taking over her chamber and packing her belongings.

Duncan had appeared in her solar, just as he'd promised, but he had brought her far more than news. He'd arrived with four maids to pack her things for a journey to his family seat.

"Nay. 'Tis madness to allow Donegal's greed to ruin a future I've sacrificed everything to secure." He pulled her out of the chamber and into the corridor, away from the din of servants' chatter and the sounds of packing.

Distracted by his words, she wondered what sacrifices he spoke of. Marriage to her? Had he bedded her for expedience's sake? She knew the answer to that, yet some long-buried part of her that had fallen for him five years ago had kept some hope alive that he would nurture some tender feeling for her. Hearing him speak of his sacrifices now dulled that hope still more.

"I cannot leave." She peered back at her solar door. "Leah sleeps in my bedchamber this night. I thought to accustom her to her new quarters before she had to move into them by herself."

She'd worried that a child used to sleeping with chamber full of her peers would feel alone and abandoned in this move intended to elevate her household status.

"The maids will not waken her. And if they do, they will be there to comfort any childish fears." He led her toward the stairs. "Come. You will find more rest this night in my chamber. We must leave at dawn."

She halted at the top step, unwilling to indulge this flight of fancy any further.

"I will not leave Domhnaill without the bonds of marriage. And there has been no talk of living at Culcanon. I have not prepared Leah for such a move. Indeed, I want her to know the security of life under this roof. She has not been raised under the most typical of circumstances."

"What child is?" Duncan turned her to hold her by the waist, inciting a riot of feeling within her from just a touch. "She will remain with us and that is as it should be."

No sooner had he dispensed with that argument than ten others arose in her mind to take its place.

"What of the danger? Don't forget your whole purpose in leaving is to make war on your brother. Why can you not do battle alone and retrieve us when it is safe?"

The line of his mouth flattened.

"And risk you using the time to make other marriage arrangements? I think not. It would be different if the priest could speak our vows in front of the whole keep before I departed, but there is not time."

Cold worry battled with the warm feelings his touch inspired even as he drew her nearer. She was not ready to leave her life behind. Besides, she did not want Leah anywhere near Donegal. She cast about wildly for another solution.

"We could speak the handfast vow before witnesses." A handfast union, while not permanently binding, was at least recognized by all the Highlands. "No man would dare touch me if we are handfasted."

"Neither will any man touch you if you are at my side every night and day." He splayed his hands along her spine, a few of his fingers sliding meaningfully between the laces of her surcoat.

And just that quickly, the fire from the night before blazed up, reminding her precisely what his hands felt like on her bare skin. The few hours they'd spent in one another's arms had outshone any idle daydream of him from her youth.

But while she trusted that Duncan would never harm her person, she did not trust that he could keep her heart safe. He'd expressed little enough interest in her wishes or her feelings on marriage. Was she no wiser than her sister to wander off into the woods with a man who was not her husband?

"Sir, you expect too much to think I will leave my father's walls with a man who has spoken no vow to me."

He shook his head.

"There is no time for the Mass your priest demands." He nudged her closer to the stairs, his hands taking liberties with her body, following the outline of her waist and hips through her garments. "But come with me now and I will speak vows about all the ways I intend to make you mine."

Duncan pressed his front to her back, whispering the last bit into her ear as he allowed her to feel the rigid, unforgiving planes of his strength. His hard male interest.

A shiver of desire coursed through her even as she knew she deserved more than this. Yet despite the soreness that remained between her thighs from the night before, she realized her body was still surprisingly responsive to his. She found herself sinking back into him, relaxing into the formidable strength that had given her such pleasure the first time.

"You are far more persuasive than you should be."
Still, she did not take that first step down the stairs.
"But why should I behave as your wife when you do
not grant me the full protection of one?"

At that, he lifted her off her feet and swept her into
his arms. In a trice, he carried her down the steps,
away from her chamber, toward the tower where he
slept.

"You have not seen my skill with a sword to make
such a naive claim. I swear on my life that I will keep
you safe." The words were the most passionate declaration he'd made toward her. Yet they were about
battle and strength. Not about tender sentiment. "And
you will be my wife tonight because you want me as
much as I want you."

Heaven help her, she could not deny it.

The need to have Cristiana had not lessened after
their one night together, Duncan realized.

Touching her once had only sharpened and intensified his appetite for more, leaving him with a fero-
cious hunger only she could tame. He pounded up the
stairs to another tower, the one where he'd slept since
arriving. It would be quieter there as he had brought
few belongings with him. There would be no packing
and preparation here.

She wound her arms about his neck, her forehead
inclined to his chin. On impulse, he lowered his lips to
kiss the top of her head where the veils did not cover

her hair. He'd shown her little enough tenderness, when he'd meant to soften her heart.

"You have put me in an untenable position, Duncan," she admitted softly as he kicked in the door to his small chamber. "As an unwed woman, I should deny you. Although as the new laird here, you may do with me as you please."

Her fingers twined through the hair at his nape, brushing the collar of his tunic. She was a warm and delectable weight against him with the side of her breast pressed to his chest and her hip fitted to his abdomen, a hair's breadth away from the tip of his raised manhood. As he angled her through the door, he dipped her body so that her soft curves grazed the swell through his garb.

"Do not fool yourself, Cristiana," he chided, amused by her dilemma. "If you did not wish to be here right now, you would let me know in no uncertain terms. You do not come to my bed because I am laird."

Someone had laid a blaze in his hearth and delivered fresh torches, illuminating the chamber far more than usual. Then again, perhaps there were servants who sought his favor now that he ruled the keep.

In the added light, he could see the becoming flush in her cheeks and the spark in her eyes as he deposited her on the bed.

"No?" The hem of her skirts billowed out about her, exposing a hint of bare calf and creamy skin.

"Nay." His mouth watered as he anticipated the taste of her. "You are here because we share something so heated and intense that it has been with us all day. Even on an afternoon when I received disturbing news, I have thought of you more than anything else."

He shed his surcoat and his tunic as if a fever gripped him. He could not recall this sense of urgency to have a woman before. Perhaps he wanted to see if this time would slake his lust in the way that their previous encounter had not. Or rather, it had more than satisfied him at the time, but he'd still left her bed already thinking about when he could return.

An odd experience for him, since carnal relations normally cleared his head.

"I spent an inordinate amount of time thinking about you, as well," she admitted, a trace of shyness in her voice.

That simple confession touched him. Reminded him that he'd vowed to be gentler with her. To soften her heart before the past returned with a vengeance.

Forcing himself to slow down, he left on his braies as he joined her on the bed that was little more than a pallet. The household servants had given him true bed linens less than a sennight prior. Stretching out to one side of her, he studied her profile in the firelight as he tugged open the laces of her surcoat.

"You enjoyed our time together?"

He loosened the laces as far as they would go,

revealing a path of white, unblemished linen from her hip to just beneath her arm. The scent of her drew him close, her fragrance bound up with layered memories of her.

"I had not imagined consummation would be so…rapturous." She peered over at him through half-lowered lashes. "It was not just pleasure. It was transforming."

Who would have guessed this woman—so recently a maid—could make his heart stutter in its rhythm? He slipped his hand beneath her loosened surcoat and atop her thin kirtle, resting his palm on the small curve of her belly.

Just above where his child might one day lay.

"It is not always like that." He did not want her to think she would feel thus if she lay in anyone else's arms. "We are more fortunate than most."

He trailed his fingers up her ribs and under her breast, where he cupped the high swell of her flesh. She made a sweetly indistinguishable noise and arched her back, pressing herself into his touch.

"Then we will have a secret recompense to a marriage of political alliance, won't we?" Through her surcoat, she covered his wandering hand with hers, steadying it where she seemed to want it the most—centered upon one breast.

He growled deep in his throat at the luscious picture she presented. Then, taxed to the end of his rope with wanting, he rose to his knees and set about pulling her surcoat up and off. She aided him, ducking and shrugging to help him in the quest. And this time, there was no maidenly shyness about leaving on her kirtle. She reached for the hem herself and edged the soft linen up her thighs. Over her hips. Off her shoulders.

Seeing her this way, fully naked and undeniably aroused, humbled him even as his body surged with the need to possess her. Her long, silken curls shielded her shoulders and framed her full breasts, the rosy color of the taut peaks mirroring the glossy mane.

"I have not visited your bed since that first night so that you might have time to heal." He smoothed her hair behind her shoulders so that he could see all of her. "I would not hurt you, lass, especially after you saw your sister callously used."

"I know that you are nothing like your brother." She lifted her hands to his chest and glided her fingertips along his skin, tantalizing him with her delicate touches. "I think it would hurt more right now if you did *not* touch me."

He had no words to answer her. Heat leaped inside him as if she'd poured some of her honeyed mead into the hearth flame.

Sitting on the side of the bed, he pulled her onto his thighs. He lowered his mouth to hers, brushing a kiss along her lips as his hands wandered the full inventory of her nakedness. He sought out every curve and hollow, leaving no place untouched, saving the sweetest parts for last. By then, she'd moved to straddle his thighs, her knees locked about his hips.

He'd thought her passionate, but he had not guessed the half of it. She had already fit herself to the bulge in his braies as if she knew exactly how to drive him out of his wits with lust. His was as sharply attuned to her as a hunter searching for his prey. The clove-and-ginger scent of her mingled with the fragrant hickory wood from the fire. The slick warmth between her legs sealed her to him, penetrating the flap of his undone braies and stiffening his shaft to unbearable proportion.

Gently, he lifted her hips. Her thighs stroked his sides while he shoved the braies down and aside, freeing himself for her. When he eased her over the swollen head, her nails dug into his shoulders, her breath catching in her throat.

He held her there for a long moment, transfixed by the way she threw her head back and rocked her hips subtly. With painstaking slowness, he filled her by degrees until sweat broke out along his brow and dusted his back. She locked her ankles behind him, holding him fast, and it took every bit of effort to rein himself in.

She was exotically beautiful in the firelight, her cinnamon hair lit with red and her skin tinged pink. But he concentrated solely on the pleasure he wanted to give her and not on all that he took. Reaching between them, he circled the sensitive nub between her legs, his finger sliding easily over her sex-slicked skin.

He watched her expression shift as he worked that tight bundle of nerves. Her brow furrowed and her lips parted. Within moments, her breasts heaved with her fast intake of breath. Sweet, mewling noises were a siren song as he changed his rhythm from slow to fast and back again.

When finally he plucked gently at her sex, she flew apart in moments. Her cries filled the room and her whole body went taut. She was wracked with wave after wave of passion, and her thighs gripped him tight, just like her womanly muscles milked his shaft within her. In no time, her movements called forth his release, his shouts overpowering hers as he flooded her with his seed.

Moments and then hours still found them twined together, their bodies perfectly fitted and in sync. They lay down together and slept, but he kept her against him long into the night.

He had expected a tug of war in bed, the same way they tussled during the day, but apparently she would not deny their attraction. She'd called this her "secret recompense" in a marriage where trust was a tenuous thing. Considering she did not know all of his secrets yet, he planned to repay her bold generosity with a thoroughness that would leave her the most well-pleasured woman in the whole of Scotland.

Chapter Ten

Cristiana debated the wisdom of riding astride on her own mount the next day. In the end, it had proven safer and faster allowing Duncan to carry Leah. Any soreness Cristiana felt from her night with the new laird was eased by the knowledge that her daughter was in the hands of the most skilled warrior in their traveling party.

Besides, Cristiana was a competent horsewoman. As children, she and her sister had loved the hunt, racing each other over hills and streams to follow their hounds or hawks. Back then, Domhnaill lands had been impenetrable, and they had been safe wherever they went.

Today, her heart seemed full of sweet recollections and memories. The whole world appeared crisper and brighter around her after the night with Duncan. The

snow tasted sweeter on her tongue. The rich color of
the horses' flanks shone deeper against the white of
the season.

"Cristiana?"

Duncan's voice called her from her thoughts and
she tugged lightly on the reins when she realized he'd
slowed his pace to speak to her.

They'd left at dawn, carrying a sleeping Leah from
her bed to join them. Their trunks were packed for a
brief stay and would follow them later. Duncan had
bid her father farewell, and the old laird had spoken
kindly enough to him. But there had been no gentle
words for her, only a stiff nod. She had hoped his
wandering mind might have forgotten the source of
his anger with her, but it seemed he remembered all
too well.

Her heart ached at the notion of leaving things that
way between them. These heightened feelings were
a double-edged sword today.

"I'm sorry." She shook her head impatiently, as if
she could ward off her worries. "My thoughts were
far away."

Her gaze dropped to Leah's sleeping form. The
child had woken a few hours ago to break her fast,
but she'd fallen back asleep shortly before the noon
sun rose to its height.

"You are not still angry that I forced you to attend
me on a journey when we are not yet wed?" Cold air
condensed in clouds as he spoke. She found herself

distracted by the movement of lips that had brought her such pleasure.

She shook her head. "I am not pleased about it, either, but I can see the wisdom of keeping Leah in your care if Donegal is resorting to the life of a brigand."

As they passed through an abandoned orchard of half-dead fruit trees, Duncan frowned, his brow heavy with concerns she understood well. Now that their futures would soon be forever linked, she had to trust he could defeat Donegal and unite their kingdoms. But would his cagey brother fall for the same kinds of deception she had when Duncan took over Domhnaill? Or would Donegal anticipate that sort of shrewdness?

Duncan ducked beneath a low limb as their mounts walked side by side. They were alone for the moment. Aside from the sleeping child in his arms, ten men rode in front of them and ten behind them. Five rode to either side of them. But the other riders were spread out over about a league, ensuring they were not set upon. Right now, Cristiana could only see the rear guard a stone's throw from them.

"So if you were not cursing your fate in making this journey, where were those faraway thoughts?" His green eyes cut to hers and he appeared genuinely interested.

"I thought of Edwina." She would not hide her affection for her sister, especially not when she had every intention of welcoming her back home, since Leah had secure protection from Donegal. "We used to ride in the hunt every fall. Father let us go all the way to this orchard. It occurred to me I'd never been so far from home. And never this far without her."

They'd been close once. Though three years apart, the two of them had thought alike. Felt alike. Neither of them had been raised with any penchant for womanly arts, eschewing embroidery for horses and hawking, mead-making and—truth be told—merry-making.

"It has always been apparent that your father is very proud of his daughters."

The notion of how betrayed her father felt tweaked her heart all over again, but she set aside that hurt to think about Edwina. Somehow, Cristiana knew her sister would return and soon. She understood it the way two close people can read each other's thoughts many leagues distant.

"From the time we were quite small, he allowed Edwina and me to remain with him at the hunters' revels afterward, leaving us alone with too much wine and mead after all the men had fallen drunk." They'd taken childish delight in pointing out which men snored the loudest or stunk the most, occasionally rearranging the mean ones in their rest in the hope they'd awaken with their fingers in their noses. "It was during those hours that we tasted and compared the unfinished brews the men left, identifying what made some palatable and others foul. I owe my success with the mead to those trips. And to Edwina, who was never afraid to grow a bit drunk herself in the pursuit of fine brew."

Belatedly, she thought of the unflattering light this might cast her sister in. But thankfully, Duncan seemed to find the story as amusing as she did, for he threw his head back and laughed. The joyful sound bounced around the limbs overhead, their world reduced to white branches and each other in a stunning expanse of trees that loomed overhead like an outdoor cathedral.

"It was said there were no maids more fearless from Angus to Buchan. And it is no wonder the daughters of Domhnaill were so well known. Your father probably played host to lords and knights up the whole coast."

"You never came," she observed lightly, drawing her cloak more tightly about her shoulders as the wind picked up and a small shower of snow fell off a tree branch.

A fleeting frown darkened his expression.

"I was fostered out to an Argyll noble." He bent over Leah's wrappings, ensuring the child was adequately covered from the elements. "I was fortunate to fight on the right side at Hastings, thanks to my overlord's kinship with a Norman. I would have left straight from there to travel the continent had my father not insisted I return home to consider marriage."

She knew how the story proceeded well enough. Despite all that had gone wrong in the latter part of their betrothal, she still had fond memories of meeting him and getting to know him. Her hand swept a spot just above her ear where he'd placed a flower once upon a time. She'd kept the dried bloom long after the man had departed.

"Your da was on my father's hunts often enough. He must not have been dissuaded by my insistence on riding with the men." She grinned over at him. "Or tasting all the leftover mead."

"Nay. Besides being complementary of your beauty, he insisted you were a maid worthy of a long journey and that I would not have his blessing for my trip abroad without seeing you first."

Her cheeks warmed to think of the Culcanon laird's kind words. There must have been a time he'd thought well of her. Too bad he hadn't had enough faith in her to believe her claims about his half brother.

"He needed you to have ties to Culcanon to ensure your return." Cristiana did not flatter herself that the old man had been particularly enamored of her. He merely knew she would make a strong political alliance for his clan.

"Whatever his reason, he made an astute choice." Duncan kept his eyes on the horizon, perhaps not intending his words to flatter her. "I had met many women in my years in Argyll and serving with the Norman, yet I could see you as my wife immediately."

This surprised her. For, although Duncan had flirted with her and given her a taste of passion with his kisses, he had never once suggested he thought they were particularly well suited.

"Yet *I* was the one who pledged my heart to you in those stolen moments when we were alone." A pledge she'd deeply regretted later when he did not care for her enough to believe her.

"Marriage is happiest when based on common interest and goals. To indulge tender feelings for one's bride is a disadvantage."

She said nothing and knew she should not be surprised. Many people thought as much. But her parents had loved each other deeply. And she'd always assumed she would wed a man who could capture her heart, as well. Even if she hadn't loved Duncan years ago, she had assumed that loving him would be inevitable. What a hollow feeling to learn he had no such aspiration. Then or now.

"But even so, I saw that you were possessed of a good heart and would make an admirable mother. You shared my dream of uniting Culcanon and Domhnaill. And you championed your sister with the same vigor that I championed the half brother I'd recently discovered."

And thus, they were back to Donegal again. At least now Duncan had seen his half sibling for the churl that he was. But that didn't mean her future husband would ever develop feelings for her that would put him at "a disadvantage."

"Forgive me if I seem impertinent, but why would you embrace him so readily?" She understood that it might be more difficult to discern shortcomings in a loved one, but she'd never comprehended Duncan's ready defense of Donegal from the first.

Besides, the horses had been ridden hard for many leagues and required the rest until—most likely—Duncan ordered another burst of speed to cover ground before the sun set.

Her only response was the crunch of the horses' hooves through packed snow for some moments. Finally, he spoke.

"Guilt, I suppose. I was provided every advantage and a thorough education as a legitimate son. Whereas Donegal received little more than rudimentary training as a warrior. I did not think it fair."

"No wonder you were so quick to give Leah a name." She remembered how resolute he'd been in that. "But not many would agree with you and defend the rights of a bastard, especially when recognizing additional children is costly."

"My father was fortunate to arrange the marriage with Edwina since our families were already in negotiations for our nuptials." Duncan turned away as his horse shook out its snow-filled mane, sending frosty bits of ice in every direction. Then, straightening,

Duncan fixed his eyes upon her. "I never understood why your father insisted that you be my bride as opposed to your sister when it is usually the eldest who makes the more substantial match. My father was unsure, as well, saying that your da was insistent on this point."

"You would have preferred Edwina." She did not have to ask. Any suitor would have favored the vibrant, older Domhnaill daughter, whose beauty was underscored by the proud tilt of her nose and the challenging light in her forward glances. "My father had grown careful with her as even his old friends noticed her, giving her unseemly looks and whispering about her bold manner. Edwina did not have the temperament to run a large household or play hostess to throngs of visitors. She did not know how to tame her wilder impulses. My father thought I would be better suited to a loftier match, though he would hardly approve Edwina going to a man without much coin. Donegal seemed like a perfect solution."

It was with a mix of pleasure and pain that Cristiana remembered her sister in those days. Edwina had been happy then, a blazing spirit that captured attention wherever she went.

"I never suggested I preferred her, only that it seemed peculiar to offer the younger daughter to the rightful laird of Culcanon. Even though Donegal was poised to receive half the lands, the laird's seat has always been destined for me." He frowned as the whirlwind of snow kicked up at the horses' hooves. "My father feared there was some sort of trickery afoot that your da was insistent upon my taking you and not Edwina, but we both agreed your disposition would serve you well as a laird's lady."

She told herself not to be incensed, but she could not help a twinge of hurt at his simple discussion of her character as if he weighed the merits of one hunting hound over another.

"Edwina never openly defied my father, but I believe he feared she could make a troublesome bride." Cristiana's heart hurt to think on it. If only their da had let her marry the man she'd once loved. "He had received another offer for her before Donegal—an offer he considered beneath her. But she cared for the suitor and complained about being denied a chance at love. On the other hand, our father relied upon me to fulfill my duty."

"Love." Duncan shook his head as if the notion were as fanciful as a child's ghost tale. "What earthly reason would she have for thinking love could be her lot?"

Cristiana bristled, her hands tightening on the reins until her horse shook his head in protest.

"We were raised by warmhearted parents who cared deeply for one another." Edwina had not been any more romantic than Cristiana. Cristiana had simply hidden her hopeful heart better.

"Tender regard can surely grow when a match is

wisely made," he assured her. He turned to the west with sudden stillness and a watchfulness came over him that she had not seen before. "Take Leah."

His words did not make sense. But the deadly seriousness of his tone and the predatory expression upon his face told her enough.

She reached for the girl as Duncan lifted her. Leah wriggled at being dislodged.

"What's amiss?" She risked a glance over her shoulder as Leah stirred and awoke.

A white cloud swirled low on the horizon, like a swirling mist in the trees.

"Enemy riders. Take cover. Fast." He kicked his horse into action, lowering his shoulders as if bracing for great speed.

Fear froze her. Where were his men to protect them?

She peered about wildly, seeing no one. Then her racing mind caught up to the direction he'd given.

"Mother, I'm thirsty," Leah complained, brushing her matted hair from her eyes as Cristiana eased her off her lap and onto the saddle.

Cristiana slid down and off the horse.

"Come. We must hide." She held her hands out to her daughter, whose eyes widened with alarm. "Bad men approach. Hurry."

The thunder of approaching hooves pounding the earth and rumbling the ground beneath their feet attested to her words. Snow fell harder from the overhead branches, the trees quaking with the deep reverberation of the oncoming riders.

Leah followed her down from the horse and then reached back for the saddlebag before Cristiana could run for a hiding place.

"We need a sword," she explained, as the bag pounded Cristiana's back with a thud.

God save them.

She would have laughed at the outrageousness of her daughter's request if she hadn't been scared to death. Sprinting through the old orchard trees, she thought hiding was useless, since the snow would show their tracks anyhow. Still, she took cover behind a thick, fallen trunk, using the travel bag as a small barricade to hide Leah on as many sides as possible. The blanket Duncan had wrapped her in was still about her shoulders, so Cristiana spread it over the girl to hide her completely.

Meanwhile, the noise of the approaching horses had slowed and changed into a clank of swords and men's shouts. Cristiana peeked over the dry, decaying bark to see Duncan circle his horse in a hard turn about an enemy rider. She could not tell how many there were as snow fell from trees and was kicked up from horses' hooves, shielding the scene in a frosty cloud. But she could see the occasional flash of steel glinting in the dull winter sun and she prayed each time that it was Duncan's sword on the winning end.

How could one man, no matter how skilled, fight off so many?

"He is a great warrior," Leah observed beside her, the child's tiny chin resting upon a smooth notch in the trunk where the bark had been stripped clean. "Is he to be my father?"

Cristiana's heart clenched at the wonder in the child's voice while Cristiana shook with fear beside her. Emotion welled up so strong and fast. Love for her daughter. Praise for the miracle of a child who could feel hope in the face of danger. Fear for the man who might never love her but who would risk his life to save her.

"God willing," she whispered, surprised at the tears burning the backs of her eyes as he drew Leah closer and squeezed. "He wishes to be your father. You see how hard he fights to protect you?"

But Leah was no longer watching. She wriggled in Cristiana's arms to see behind them.

"Look, Mother!" she whispered excitedly, pointing to the south.

Riders flying the Culcanon standard bore down on them. Her heart dropped as she recalled King Malcolm's letter that accused Donegal of fighting under Duncan's standard. Could the half brother's forces attack them from two sides?

"Get down," Cristiana ordered, shoving Leah safely back under the blanket as she searched the saddlebag for a weapon.

There was no sword, of course, but there was a small dagger. Cristiana withdrew it, planning to use it on anyone who tread close enough to touch them. Anyone who threatened Leah would have to shed blood before to see it through.

She vowed if they made it out of this alive, she would not yearn for love in her marriage any longer.

But remaining dispassionate about a man who would lay down his life for Leah would not be easy.

Duncan fought the final man to the ground, leaving him with a wound to the thigh that would not permit him to remount.

The mist of snow cleared now that all the horses had run off save his. There had only been four men to stave off, their numbers having been initially decreased by the men-at-arms that had guarded the west flank of the traveling party. Duncan had not recognized them. If Donegal was assembling bands of brigands to thieve the king and harass travelers, he was not using men from Culcanon lands.

Turning, Duncan peered back to the east, to where he'd left Cristiana and the little sprite. He saw Cristiana's horse rooting about the snow for grass, unconcerned with the turmoil nearby.

Behind the palfrey, however, the scene was not so tame. Riders bearing the Culcanon banner circled the place in the forest where Cristiana should be. But this was not any of Duncan's men. He knew from the spears they carried—simple weapons that were not the kinds of arms his men had brought on this journey.

The sweat had not begun to dry on his back from the first battle. He could not possibly take on so many and win.

Still, he could not allow them to take the women without a fight. Rage flared in his chest, his anger spurring his heels as he urged his mount toward those menacing riders. Where in Hades were his men? And how big was this group that attacked them?

From the corner of his vision, he spotted movement from the north. Even without turning, he knew these riders were his men. To an ear long trained to distinguish the sounds of war, the cacophony of his knights speeding over the landscape was as unique as a babe's cry to its mother. There was a snap to Harold's rich cloak in the wind, a hissing whip of Gerard's sword as he rode with it already poised for striking, a jangle to John the Fat's spurs. Duncan raised his own sword to ensure the men recognized him and understood Cristiana was surrounded by traitors.

He lifted a war cry to the heavens, bellowed from the soles of his feet. His men picked up the battle cry as they rode in from the north, their voices magnifying his and filling the glade with an ancient warning. Not even the heathen Vikings had misunderstood it when Duncan's ancestors unleashed the predatory call on the invading Norsemen.

The throng of enemy riders seemed to take their measure, their helm-covered heads whipping about to see from whence the sound came and—perhaps—attempting to gauge the size of the oncoming threat. At the center of the riders, on the ground, he spied Cristiana.

Defiant and proud, she stood alone.

Where was Leah?

Had they already taken the child? He rechanneled the chill of fear into propelling strength. Coaxing one last burst of speed from his warhorse, Duncan set his course for the south end of the circle, helping his men to pen the enemy in. They could retaliate with a threat to Cristiana, but they were already too late. Duncan's best crossbow shooter had already felled two of the enemy.

In a desperate retreat, the remaining riders fled to the east, their horses kicking up snow and dirt. Cristiana sank to the ground, throwing herself on a pile of blankets.

A heap of wriggling blankets. Reining in his destrier, Duncan reached her first and spied Leah emerging from the dark woolen covering that had hidden her from the enemy.

Never in all his days had he felt relief so strong. The force of it almost knocked him from his mount. Cristiana was safe. Leah remained safe.

In all the ways that counted, the two females cling-ing to each other and crying in the orchard were his family now.

After a quick gesture to his men to secure the perimeter and account for the fallen, Duncan slid to the ground to pull Cristiana and her daughter into his arms. His child now. He needed to feel them, warm and alive.

"You are unharmed." He drew Cristiana close and kissed the top of her head.

Stiffening, she straightened and clutched Leah tighter. Her icy glare was unmistakable.

Apparently, she did not share his gratitude at find-ing her betrothed alive.

"This is a fool's errand and I will attend you no longer." She kept her voice low so Leah would not hear. "Those men were armed to the teeth and they sought something they could not find. Whether they have heard rumors about Leah or not, I cannot say. But I insist we return to Domhnaill at once."

Chapter Eleven

She had not won her way.

Cristiana paced outside the Culcanon great hall, where Duncan had been shut in with his men every since they'd arrived at his family's stronghold. She had never visited this keep before, but even she could tell the fortress had been recently picked clean of its treasures. There were shadows on the walls showing the outlines of where tapestries had recently hung and fresh gouges in the heavy timber fortifications where iron torch holders had been pried loose from their settings. Metalwork of some sort had been torn off the dais table in the hall—something she'd seen in the brief moments she'd had a glimpse of that space before a maid showed her to a small quarter for Leah.

Her daughter had been happy to meet other children. The Culcanon keep was home to several boys and girls close to her in age. Leah had quickly joined a group of young girls who'd been sharing a doll and cakes by a warm hearth.

And while Cristiana had been pleased that her daughter could adjust so easily to new surroundings, Cristiana had been reluctant to follow the maid to the laird's chamber, where her things were already being unpacked.

Apparently, no one thought twice about installing Cristiana in the laird's bed even though she'd exchanged no wedding vows with Duncan. Instead, she'd watched over the corridor outside the great hall, waiting to give him a piece of her mind.

She must have fallen asleep in the chair where she sat near a family of cats prowling the hall in search of dinner. The small candle she'd set beside her on a table in the corridor burned low by the time Duncan emerged. It had to be past midnight. All her feline companions snoozed contentedly near her feet.

"You must be exhausted," Duncan announced, his eyes raking over her as she stood.

Oddly, her skin warmed as if he'd touched her. How could her body respond to him so immediately, even when her brain had warned her how dangerous entangling her heart would be?

"I am not too tired to force you to hold up your end of our bargain." She scooped her small candle off the table and blew it out, unwilling to part with precious beeswax in a keep where torches were few and far between. "You promised you would keep Leah safe, and given how unstable your relations are with Donegal, that means allowing her to return to Domhnaill."

She pressed the candle into her palm, careful to keep the melted wax in its well until it cooled and hardened.

"Did I not prove today that she is better off close to me? And I must be here."

"Donegal will not attack Domhnaill." She and Leah would be safest there.

For that matter, Cristiana's heart would be safest there, as well. She could not fall prey to Duncan's appeal if she was many leagues apart from him. Perhaps the time away would help her to shore up her defenses against him. She might have allowed him into her keep, but she still had the option of barring her heart from his disarming smile.

"Donegal will raid wherever I am not." He gestured expansively to the defaced walls all around them, the torch he carried flaring as he drew it through the air. "He is not afraid to accost the king's men. What makes you think he will quail at the sight of Domhnaill walls, especially when he has every reason to bear your father a grudge."

"My father?" The notion surprised her more than anything, but she could understand his reasons immediately.

"He withheld Donegal's betrothed. No matter how you view it or how your father viewed their early consummation, the vast majority of overlords in the land would have enforced the bridal contract. Can we agree on that much at least?"

Unsure of herself, she recalled the feeling of helplessness today in the orchard and knew she must listen to Duncan's counsel. Whether she willed it or nay, Duncan's sword arm and battle strategy were her best defense for Leah.

She shook her head mutely.

"Come." He enveloped her in one thick arm and guided her toward the stairs. "You must rest."

Foreboding forced her feet to be still on the cold stone floor.

"I cannot take up residence in your chamber without having submitted to a priest's blessing."

"By the saints, you are stubborn." Duncan handed her the torch and, thinking he meant to send her off to another chamber on her own, she took it. Of course, he proceeded to sweep her off her feet and carry her in the direction she'd refused to walk. "I claimed you and Leah as my own in front of every noble of note at Domhnaill before your guests departed for their homes. We are already wed in the ways that count."

Knowing she was too tired to think straight, Cristiana argued no more. Her head lolled to the side, resting on his shoulder in spite of herself.

"I will make a stronger case tomorrow morning, perhaps."

"You will be too enamored of my lovemaking tomorrow morning to argue."

Desire curled through her like the wisps of smoke spiraling off the torch flame as they moved through the deserted keep. Everyone but his men seemed to be fast asleep, and they'd left the knights behind in the great hall to bed down on the floor.

"You do not command me," she reminded him, feeling too helpless by half.

"Lucky for me, no commands will be required." His grip tightened on her thigh as he cradled her to his chest.

With his other hand, he spanned the side of her rib cage, his fingers straying close to the softness of her breast. Because she held the torch aloft, she had no defense against the subtle roaming of his palms.

Heaven help her, her whole body hummed with anticipation of more of that touch. As he hurried his pace up the squat, dark tower's steps, a medallion at his neck slid free of his tunic, the metalwork intricate and heavy.

"I have seen you wear this often," she remarked, her face still burning from his blatant sensual threat. She was not sure if she wished to distract him from touching her tonight, but she did not think she could discuss what they were about to do in the open manner that he could. "Is it a family piece?"

"It is the map to the Viking treasure. I have been meaning to show it to you." He told her, his expression utterly solemn as he reached a huge door at the top of the stairwell. Even here, the ironwork had been removed from the door, as had the torch well. Rough-hewn planks served as reinforcements to the entry now.

"You're serious." She did not try to hide her surprise. "You honestly believe an ancient treasure hides at Domhnaill?"

She lowered the torch as he kicked open the door and brought her through the archway. Vaguely, she noticed the stark emptiness of the chamber that might have been lush at one time. Rough linens and a woolen coverlet had been thrown over the bed.

He settled her on the center of the pallet carefully, mindful of the torch in her hand. He took it from her and deposited the base into crudely fashioned iron ring that appeared newly installed. A low fire had been laid in the hearth, but with the walls robbed of tapestries, the chill in the chamber was fierce.

"Of course there is a treasure. Were you not raised on the same tales that I was told?" He opened a trunk at the end of the pallet and pulled a heavy fur cloak from within. Wrapping it about her shoulders, he bent close, his cheek next to hers as he drew the excess over her legs.

"An ancient laird hid his riches in the forest after a lookout spotted invader ships on the horizon."

"Aye. He was the last laird to rule both Domhnaill and Culcanon lands, but he fled the larger Domhnaill keep and retreated to this fortress, which he kept manned until the end Danes were so intermarried they were as much native as pagan." Satisfied that he'd swathed her sufficiently in the fur, Duncan set to work tugging Cristiana's hair out from under the cloak to flow over her shoulders and down her back. "In truth, I am more Domhnaill than you since my forebears were the original Saxon overlords while your ancestors were the heathen Norse."

She smiled at his teasing words, grateful for the momentary distraction from the scent of him surrounding her in the folds of his cloak.

"Not too heathen." Lifting a lock of her red-gold hair, she waved it for emphasis. "It seems the Scots left their stamp upon me."

He took up the lock of hair and twined it about his finger.

"There is red there, true. But 'tis mingled with Danish gold."

His gaze dipped to her mouth. For a moment, she thought he would kiss her. Indeed, she wanted the taste of him upon her lips. But then he released her hair and edged back from her again.

Her heart beat so rapidly she feared he would see the erratic pulse at her neck. She burrowed her chin into the fur collar to hide her response.

"But you asked about this," he continued, easing

the chain over his head before he handed the heavy ornament to her. "I found it when I returned to Culcanon to gather my forces. I had heard Donegal let the men's training lapse and that he used the resources of the keep to fight his own battles. I did not realize how grave the situation was until I returned to see the riches of the keep sold off and the people starving. I had been away too long, serving the king, putting my faith in a man who shared my blood."

The dark glower upon his brow told her he still did not fathom the defection. But then, how could a man of honor understand the heart of one so traitorous?

She bent her head close to his, warmed inside that he would take this time to speak with her rather than drawing her straight into his bed. Could they develop some bond beyond the heat that sparked between them?

"But the king rewards you well by entrusting you with Domhnaill." She knew her keep was worth far more than his. If outside forces had not set them at odds, it would have been a wise match.

His expression shifted. Inscrutable green eyes met hers. Looked away.

"The king did not give me anything I did not already plan to take."

She was not sure why he felt the need to make the distinction. Did he hope to remind her of his traitorous entry with his request for Christian mercy?

"But you have admitted you had no resources and

your people went hungry. How do you think you could have beaten our defenses when—"

"It is over." He cut her off abruptly, his tone hard and unyielding. "We spoke of the medallion."

"Did we?" Cristiana tried to refocus her attention, but old anger still simmered. Perhaps another woman could have bit back her pride with ease, but Cristiana had run Domhnaill long enough to know their battle strength. Did Duncan think her naive enough to believe he could have stormed those gates successfully?

"Yes." He bit off the word and busied himself with removing his boots, almost as if he wrestled with a frustration as great as hers. "I found it when I inspected some of the damage done to the metalwork above the hearth in the great hall. Donegal had sold the hammered metal frontispiece proclaiming the family name. Behind it, the stonework crumbled and I ordered mortar to fix it. But as the workers cleared the debris, they discovered this hidden behind the fallen stones."

Intrigued, Cristiana took a closer look at the heavy silver ornament he'd handed her. It had been designed in an ancient style, with the exotic knots and endless interweaving of animal's bodies that sometimes appeared on old gravestones or upon church decoration. "It is obviously very old." She ran her fingers over a series of notched markings. "Is this damage from the workers' axes?"

Duncan watched with relief as the artifact absorbed her attention. He did not wish to dwell on the matter of Malcolm's ruling on Domhnaill, which had not been a decree that Cristiana wed him so much as an offering of royal support to aid Culcanon's recovery from the damage done under his brother's steward-ship. The news that Duncan had used the letter as leverage to press marriage would not be happily met by his betrothed, especially in light of his takeover of the keep through intrigue.

One day, he would help her to see the merit of a bloodless coup. But he planned to delay that day until her heart had softened toward him. Or at least until their wedding vows had been issued before the priest.

"Those are not new marks," he answered her, enclosing his hand about hers to guide her finger over the notches she'd noticed. "They are ancient letters. Rune markings. They say 'Look east when Domhnaill finds his way home.'"

Cristiana moved her finger off the time-worn markings to peer at the runes. Duncan kept his hand about hers, however, savoring the soft feel of her skin against his palm. His chest pressed against her back as he leaned close. The sweet scent of her mead-making had not left her, not even this far from the home where her brews awaited her. Unable to resist, he lowered his nose to her hair and inhaled the cinnamon and ginger spice that clung to her.

"Look east?" She peered back at him, brow furrowed. "I do not understand. Are you suggesting the treasure is in the sea?"

"Nay." He closed her hand about the medallion again and turned it. "You see these headings about the perimeter?"

He turned her shoulders with his to help the hearth light reach the silver piece. His heartbeat surged with the want of her. He could not understand how his desire for her grew each time he was with her—until it increased to a sharp, persistent longing.

"Yes!" She turned to him, excitement plain in her animated gaze. "The fur and feathers of the animals contain the directions of the map."

"You know Latin?"

The letter for *east* was not a rune but a Latin notation. Not even Duncan had been educated in the language.

"Nay." She shook her head even though she had deciphered the letter clearly enough. "Only what I have learned at Mass."

Clearly, he needed to pay more attention to the priest.

"All of this is Latin, as well." He pointed to the small fins on a fish that appeared to be decorative markings unless you studied it carefully. "It suggests the design is a map of a Domhnaill landmark and the words end with—"

"Culcanon." Cristiana nodded. "I have seen the

name written before. Culcanon of Domhnaill would have been the laird who hid the treasure before fleeing here."

"Aye." Gently, he pried the medallion from her fingers and set it aside. "But you may study it tomorrow. You must be weary from the ride."

Seeing her face down his enemies today had left him more shaken than he could have ever guessed. Part of it was because he would be left with a child to raise when he had hardly gotten to know Leah. But there was more to it than that. He'd felt a strong urge to hack down any man who neared Cristiana of Domhnaill, and it was an impulse that went deeper than possessiveness.

He needed to be careful of her affect on him.

"I am." She nodded, but did not make any move to lie down.

"You will sleep here tonight," he warned, unwilling to indulge her on this.

She nodded. "I was just thinking how grateful I am that you were not lying about the treasure at least. It has been difficult to put my faith in you after what took place between our families. So I am pleased to learn you did not invent the story of the treasure hunt merely as an entertainment for my court."

Ah, the arrow of her gratitude stung his conscience. Tomorrow, he would call his priest and secure the marriage. Tomorrow, he would untwine the lies that remained between them.

But for tonight, he could do naught but guide her sleep form down to the soft pallet and provide his arm for her pillow.

"Come. You are too weary for me to touch you as I would like. Rest now."

She was asleep almost instantly, leaving him with a confusion of thoughts as he watched the measured rise and fall of her breasts. He loosened her surcoat, but only to make her more comfortable while she slept.

He had ignored his desires for her sake. And while he'd like to think that was a bit of noble restraint on his part, he feared the larger part of his reason for holding back was the growing tenderness he felt for her. And no matter how much he admired her, he would now allow himself to care about a woman who could turn off her feelings for him at a moment's notice. She had done so five years ago after they'd shared kisses and she'd made sweet promises to him.

She could do it again.

This time, Duncan would not feel the sting of betrayal. Because this time, he had no intention of losing his heart to the enemy.

She played a dangerous game.

Edwina hastened her pace to keep up with Henry as his boots thundered through the courtyard of a rugged coastal fortress far south of Domhnaill. Three days had passed since she'd convinced him to bring her north under the pretense of a marriage she had no intention of making. But now that she was out of Evesburh and could claim no protection, save this young knight's, she had renewed appreciation for how utterly dependent upon him she would be until they reached Domhnaill.

"Henry, wait." Her hands were raw from guiding the reins on a horse too spirited for a woman who hadn't ridden in years. Her clothes were mud-spattered, the cloak torn in two places from tree branches they'd encountered during the ride. She'd insisted on riding her own mount so they could make better time, but since winning that battle, Henry had not been easily managed for days.

Now, he either ignored her or did not hear her as he was so far ahead. Dropping all pretense of dignity as she neared the rich, stone fortress alive with light and activity, Edwina pulled up her skirts and ran to catch up.

"Henry, please." Out of breath, she inserted herself between him and the door to the keep.

They'd been admitted to the courtyard by a surly guard at a watchtower, the bridge to the main keep open even though they'd been warned it would be closed for the night in another hour.

"Edwina, we must hurry unless we want to spend the night, and I do not welcome the prospect of so many hours in a Scots' stronghold while I bear William's standard."

"Scots?" She peered around the courtyard at the scurrying grooms and maids, the swaybacked farm horses plodding past well-dressed destriers on their way to and from the stables. "We have crossed the border?"

She had seen no change in landscape, no boundary marking. Somehow, she'd always imagined she would sense a change in the air when she returned to her homeland. In her memory, the air had been far sweeter in the land of the Scots.

"Aye." He gripped her shoulders and eased her aside, taking advantage of his surprise. "I wish to obtain a safe passage from the king before we travel any farther."

Edwina was not sure why Malcolm would be in residence here, far from his family seat, but then she had not kept abreast of foreign politics while at William's court.

Following Henry into the entry, she was treated to an immediate view of the hall, where the king's shield rested against the dais.

By the saints.

The man with more power than any to punish Donegal the Foul was present this night. Her thoughts racing for how to approach him—how to make an appeal for punishment—she stood frozen. Now that she'd spent time among William's court, she knew anyone could at least ask the king for his justice. She was no innocent country maid content to abide her father's rulings anymore. She could obtain justice here. Now.

"Come, Edwina." Henry urged her forward, sliding an arm about her waist. "We will obtain safe passage at the same time we receive his blessing for our marriage. We can be on our way to Domhnaill this very night."

"No." She halted again, the potential disaster of the situation finally revealing itself. "Nay, Henry, we cannot."

This time she caught *him* off guard, yanking him into the shadows of the corridor outside the open hall.

His frown did not dissuade her. If ever there had been a time for honesty, this was it. She did not have enough time to think through an elaborate scheme. Besides, Henry deserved better than more pretty lies.

"We cannot wed. I have been more wronged than you can imagine by someone who was once close to me and my heart is too filled with bitterness to love."

His frown deepened. "I brought you all this way. You promised—"

"I made no promise, Henry." The depth of her wretchedness pained her as she watched his face twist in confusion. "You are too good of a man to hurt this way, yet I could not have trusted any other to deliver me safely home."

"We are not at Domhnaill yet. You are tired. You are not thinking clearly."

"No. I have deceived you most unkindly because life has made me an exile and an outcast. My heart has hardened—" She gasped, her hand moving to cover the vital organ she had just dismissed as toughened beyond penetration.

"What is it?" Henry peered over his shoulder to see what had caught her attention.

How could he possibly understand? Even she did not believe what she spied with her own eyes.

Cullen of Blackstone had just risen from a seat somewhere in the great hall to pass into her view. He approached the king's table, tall and lean with the uncanny grace of a forest creature that would make him appear young long after his hair turned gray.

"I—" Her voice cracked before she could form an answer. Heaven help her, she had never expected to see Cullen again. "There are so many ghosts of my past here." She needed to retreat. She could not face the king with Cullen there, reminding her of long-forgotten dreams and piercing her heart with all that could never be. Overcome with emotion, she gripped Henry's arms. "You have been too kind and, I swear, if you will attend me on my journey north, I will find you the most dazzling bride you've ever seen. A young, innocent lass—"

"It is *you* that I want, Edwina." In the half-light of the corridor, with the torches flickering shadows across his face, Henry did not appear so youthful. The dark growth of a beard from days on the road hid the pockmarks of his cheek. Oh, he was a handsome one after all and would be more so with age.

"I love another," she confessed, unwilling to lead him astray even one more moment. She had not even admitted it to herself, but right now, she forced the truth from her lips in penance for what she'd done to a noble, upstanding man. "I can never be with him for he is a nobleman and I'm a ruined woman. There was a time when I was above him in station but loved him anyway. My father would not allow me to wed him, giving me instead to a brute that defiled me before the vows." She blinked hard, hating that she sounded so young and foolish. Of course, she *had* been young and foolish. She had tried to make the best of her betrothal to Donegal, hoping that stolen kisses with him could compare to the secret trysts she'd once shared with Cullen.

Never had she been more wrong about anything.

A helpless cry of regret edged from her throat, echoing through the foyer. Henry shushed her, his expression half sympathetic and half horrified.

Her eyes lingering on her long-ago love, Edwina allowed the old hurt to wash over her a moment longer before she willed it away. She had worked too hard to get here to fall apart now. The king sat so near.

"I must speak my peace." Breaking away from Henry, she strode into the great hall.

Her torn cloak and mud-stained skirts dragged heavily through the rushes where she tread. Head held high, she let her hood fall, revealing the red-gold locks that remained her best feature. Keeping her gaze trained on the king, she ignored the murmurs at her arrival and the sound of Henry's hurried step behind her.

"Edwina?" Cullen's voice found her ears when she was deaf to all else.

She could not read the nuance of the sound—if he was simply surprised or disparaging. Unwilling to think about that now, she curtsied deeply before the dais.

Mindful of Cullen's eyes upon her, Edwina humbled herself before Malcolm.

"If it pleases you, my lord, I have traveled far to seek the king's justice."

Chapter Twelve

"You cannot keep me here forever."

Cristiana paced the laird's chamber three nights after arriving at Culcanon, frustrated and restless from the days of inactivity. She missed her father and her people. She wondered about various batches of mead that needed ingredients added. Most of all, she worried that if Edwina returned home she would wonder where Cristiana had gone.

After her initial letter to Edwina, Cristiana realized her error in assuming Edwina could simply return home. She'd sent a second missive with enough coin to secure safe passage, but with no word from her sister after so many days, she feared her letters had not arrived.

"You are hardly my prisoner." Duncan traced the

engraving on his medallion to provide her with a copy to study.

She still could not imagine a treasure hidden on Domhnaill lands, but she had not studied the cryptic map for long, either. Duncan wore it about his neck at all times, and the sorry state of his keep ensured he was busy every moment of each day.

Even the nights had not brought them close. He returned to his chamber long after she slept and was up before she rose in the morning.

Until this night. He'd intercepted her in the hall after she'd spent the evening with some of the other women, applying her woeful embroidery skills to a new tapestry for Duncan's chamber.

"It feels like a prison," she remarked, circling the chamber while he worked, her gaze taking in the remnants of kitchen leftovers he'd carried up with him. The mead of Culcanon was truly dreadful. "Leah does not mind it, but I do not wish to be here and have no way to return home unless you accompany us."

He set aside the tracing to give her his full attention. When his green eyes settled on her, she realized this was what she'd wanted. His attention. His eyes upon her like a caress.

She shivered and tried to hide it. How much might it hurt to care about him again? To feel the sting of betrayal again? Ah, it was unwise to have sought his interest tonight.

"You know we need to find Donegal before he

hurts anyone else. He is paying an army of miscreants with misbegotten gains from my keep." He gestured to the bare walls.

She said nothing, unsure how to proceed. Speak her peace? Or continue accepting whatever pretense of a betrothal he offered? No doubt, her marriage would not thrive on secrets and lies.

"We did not plan for such obstacles when we discussed what marriage would be like that first time." Folding her arms across her chest, she neared the fire to warm herself and so she did not have to see his expression. Would he think her remembrances foolish? Did he disdain her soft-hearted memories of the past?

He said nothing. She wondered what he was thinking. Did he recall the same sweetness between them that she did? Or had his wooing of her merely been his way of sweetening a betrothal that neither of them had any great say in?

"Do you remember?" Her voice hit an odd note. "It was so long ago that we spoke of our future together. Perhaps you've forgotten."

Perhaps that discussion hadn't been nearly as memorable for him as it had been for her. Surely, it was weakness to raise the issue at all and prove to him she thought back to such things. But if there was to be any animosity between them, she would prefer to understand his position rather than guess at the boundaries of his resentments.

He pounded his fist on the table so hard his medallion jumped. So did she. She turned to see his hand still clenched on the rough-hewn plank.

"You think I would forget that?" he demanded, his voice low and angry.

Nay, offended.

Rising from his chair, his presence seemed to fill the chamber.

"I do not know what is important to you and what isn't." Shrugging, she held her hands out helplessly. "It's hard for me to tell what you think is significant enough to remember."

"I remember every moment and every word exchanged that day." The shadows under his eyes were from lack of sleep, but they gave his visage a lean, dangerous look. "My first day back at Domhnaill, I went in search of the place we kissed and—"

Her cheeks burned as he left the sentence unfinished. She had allowed him too many liberties that day as a hopeful, lovesick maid. But then she had wondered about passion ever since her older sister had admitted to trysts with Cullen of Blackstone before their father had refused his suit. Edwina had spoken so fervently about the feel of a man's arms, that Cristiana had been eager to experience such things for herself.

Duncan's hands and mouth had proved her undoing the day they'd stolen away from the keep.

"I thought we were to wed." Otherwise, she would

have never allowed her surcoat to fall away from her breasts the way it had that day. "We were but days away from speaking the vows."

"Do you know what happened when I searched for that place where I touched you and you promised to warm my heart and my bed for all time?"

Her whole body flamed to have her words spoken back to her so bitingly. She'd given herself too freely, never guessing he could turn on her so easily.

"We built the mead house upon that spot." She knew exactly what had become of the place where she'd come so unwound in this man's arms. "I did not want to see our glade and remember how foolish I'd been."

Some of the tension in his shoulders seemed to relax as his expression cleared.

"Yet you stand on that very spot every day, do you not? Perhaps you did not bury the glade so much as you commemorated it."

She shook her head. "Nay. I did not want to remember."

"But you do. We both do." He stepped closer, his hold on her in the present as powerful as the grip he'd always had in her memory, even though he did not touch her.

"We have lost so much." She could not begin to compare the loss of her starry-eyed youth to all her sister had lost. But they'd both had an innocence taken from them by the Culcanons. "I thought you would stand by me."

"I thought you would honor your promises. But if we brood about all we've lost, we will never find any contentment in marriage. Can we not celebrate what is left to us?"

Trembling with too much emotion, she stood before him, searching his eyes for some hint of his meaning. Even with the hearth fire at her back and the fiery heat of his body in front of her, she still felt a chill deep inside.

"What is left when trust and hope have fled?"

"You can rebuild trust with time." He took her hand and folded it inside his. Then he lifted her palm to his chest and placed it there, above his heart.

Frustration edged out some of the hope she'd felt.

"I do now know how."

"You have already witnessed my commitment to keep my vow to protect Leah. With my life, I have kept her safe."

She nodded, remembering how scared she'd been and how fearlessly Duncan had placed himself between Leah and danger. There were some things she could not do for Leah, some things only Duncan could provide in this harsh land they called home.

"Now it's your turn," he continued. "You can make good on a vow to me."

Stepping closer, he sealed her body to his, molding her curves to fit against him.

Still, she remained silent. Mute in the face of the passion she'd never been able to rein in with him. Breathless from the feel of him, she curled her fingers about his shoulders.

He slid one palm inside the slashed sleeve of her surcoat and used the leverage to tug the overdress down one shoulder, baring a patch of skin at her neck to his avid gaze.

"You promised once to warm my bed forever. You can start this night."

He knew without question she would come to him.

He preferred that she do so because she wanted to. Because she regretted the way she had gone back on her word five years ago.

He'd stayed away from her for days, giving her time to make peace with the marriage he'd offered her no say in. By tonight, he'd known she would never come to him freely without something to drive her into his arms. When he had plotted to win Domhnaill, he had not counted on how much he would want to win her.

"I am in no position to deny you." She licked her lips, taking no responsibility for her own desire even though her fingers sank into his skin and her heart pounded so hard he could feel it through his tunic.

The skin in the hollow of her neck pebbled where he'd kissed it.

"But I've made no demand." It took considerable will to hold back for as long as he had. A vein in his temple throbbed with the effort.

Letting her go now could be his undoing, but he was prepared to do so. He needed her to admit this heat between them was not one-sided.

Still she said nothing. A silent battle of will and want.

So, against every instinct he possessed, he forced himself to relinquish his hold. Regret burned his throat. His breath whooshed in and out of his lungs like a warhorse after battle.

The confusion in her lovely gray eyes would have given him more satisfaction if he had not been burning from the inside out. Her lips parted. In protest?

"You are wicked to the very core," she accused softly, taking the smallest of steps toward him. "Do not leave me."

Untwining the clasp on her girdle, she let the jeweled belt fall to the floor. His eyes followed the movement, hardly daring to believe she would offer herself to him. And that's what she did—by deed if not word.

It was his turn to remain silent. Not because he waged that battle of will anymore. Rather, the sight of her unfastening the laces of her garb and lifting the heavy fabric up and off had robbed him of the ability to speak.

"You have shown me delights I never imagined." The soft fabric of the kirtle clung to her curves, revealing more than it concealed. "They have worked a magic on my soul that won't free me even when you release me."

He reached out to her then, drawing close the soft, fragrant warmth of her. Lowering his mouth to hers, he nipped her bottom lip, then kissed the same place.

"You seem to have spoken my thoughts for me." He wrapped his arms about her, splaying his hand along her back and shoulders in order to touch as much of her as he could. "I feel those things, too."

Arching up on her toes, she fitted herself against him. Her eagerness stoked the fire within and he rent the sheer fabric of her kirtle in his haste to feel her skin.

Her hands were no more patient than his, her fingers working the ties of his tunic, then falling to the lacing of his braies. She went back and forth, tugging knots into them that hadn't been there before, her thighs moving restlessly between his as she hummed frustrated noises against his neck where she laid kisses.

"Let me." He took over the job, freeing himself of his garb in moments, knots and all.

She watched him in the firelight, her gaze bold

and appreciative, devoid of self-consciousness. But then, this was what had fascinated him about her ever since his father had written about her. Cristiana of Domhnaill had no use for feminine pretense or false modesty. She thirsted for adventure, knowledge and passion. Maybe now that she did not have so many secrets to keep, she would find her way back to her passions.

"No woman's gaze has ever flattered me so well." He ached for the want of her.

A smile curved her lips as she reached for his hip. Her hand stroked him there, just beside the hard, heavy weight that craved her the most.

"No man has ever allowed me such liberties," she whispered, finally switching her attention from his hip to the throbbing length of him.

Her teasing words stirred a possessive storm within him even as her finger traced the thick, corded vein down the front of his shaft.

"And now, no other man will ever dare to try." He charged her, backing her to his bed and tumbling her down to the pallet. Though he protected her back with his hand, he was careful not to put his full weight on her as they landed.

That fall seemed to crumble the last of his restraints. He explored every curve and hollow with his hands, kissing and tasting his way down her body, pausing at the places that made her squirm and gasp with pleasure. He would not disappoint her now that she had confessed her desire for him. He would make this night the most fulfilling to show her they were meant to be together. That they never should have been apart.

"Duncan!" She cried out a breathy plea as his kisses strayed below her navel.

Her fragrance surrounded him, intensified by the heat of her skin, and mingled with the scent of her hunger. Her fingers scratched softly at his shoulders, her hips rolling with each flick of his tongue along her taut belly.

When he parted her thighs and placed that first kiss against the slickness he discovered there, she would have bolted upright if not for his steadying hand on her hip. Her protest was all innocent distress without any teeth, for she settled into the pallet easily enough after a few more strokes of his tongue against the tight bud of her sex. The sound of throaty approval she made urged him on in spite of her restless wriggling.

He lost himself in the taste and feel of her. As much as he wanted to sink into her and remember that sweet tightness all around him, he wanted this for her more. He couldn't wait to feel her pleasure this way, to know he'd taken her somewhere she'd never been before.

He was so wrapped up in providing that high that he must have missed the warning signs. Her body went as taught as a bowstring, her muscles straining with unnatural stillness for a long moment until she flew apart beneath him.

Her sex throbbed as she let the waves of bliss roll over her. He did not release her until she'd been still for a long time, making sure he'd teased every last lush contraction from her passionate body.

He stretched out over her, settling himself between her thighs, playing in the slick sweetness he found there.

"I need you," he admitted, unable to hold back his own desires. "Now."

With a wordless nod, she shifted, helping him be right where he wanted. Sweetly, she lifted her hips, giving him access to everything he needed.

He entered her in one smooth stroke, seating himself fully inside her. Little spasms leftover from her release squeezed him, teasing him with what was to come.

"Let me be on top," she whispered in his ear, so softly he thought he might have misheard.

But when he reared back to look in her eyes, there could be no mistake. Cristiana wanted her adventure. And hadn't he promised himself she could have it this night?

"Now who is the wicked one?" He smiled at her boldness even as he rolled onto his back, allowing her to do with him as she wished.

She moved awkwardly at first, unsure how to obtain what she wanted. But soon, she found ways to move that seemed to please her. And he would have found a whole lot of joy just in watching her please herself, but somehow all the things that felt good to her felt cursedly perfect to him, too.

Although he loved watching her astride him, her chin tilted up and her lips parted in sensual surprise, he had to close his eyes to fight off his release for as long as he could. He would not rob her of pleasure any sooner than he had to.

But try as he might, he could not stave off the heat building within him. Her slender thighs worked it out of him, her beautiful body coaxing a shuddering climax from his. He howled with the force of it, wrapping his arms about her and pulling her down to his chest.

"You are mine." He spoke the words hoarsely into her ear, possessiveness gripping him as tightly as the woman herself.

But no matter how fiercely he told himself that Cristiana belonged to him forever, he could not help the warning voice in his head that told him the opposite was just as true.

He belonged to her. Despite his best intentions, he'd allowed her to slip past his guard to settle in his heart all over again.

"Edwina."

The masculine voice reverberated through her whole body, the sound humming sweetly in her veins as she made her way through the dank and cheerless Scots stronghold where Malcolm was in residence.

Edwina had obtained some justice from the king—his word that Donegal would be punished. But Malcolm had not commanded a force of riders to hunt down the weasel-faced rat, so her victory had been less satisfying than she'd hoped.

Now, she faced a night alone in this friendless place, without a protector, since Henry had been ordered to attend the Scots king this night. Perhaps that meant Malcolm expected him to raise a drinking horn with the other men. More likely, he intended to send the young knight home.

Leaving her alone to greet the man she longed—and feared—to see again.

Turning on her heel, she met his gaze as boldly as she could manage. There was no use hiding how she'd fallen in the world. He surely knew all about her exile. Perhaps he thought it well-deserved given the way she had not fought harder for love. For him.

But it had been her father's decision to refuse his suit. Her father who had wanted a more lucrative alliance for Domhnaill than Cullen had been able to provide. With all her heart, she had the strong, quiet knight who had balanced her adventurous spirit so well. Once her father said no, however, what else could she have done? Cullen had disappeared from her world, leaving her with only memories of their time together.

"Cullen." Her voice almost wavered on that one word. She tilted her chin higher. Prouder.

His face was no less dear for the new lines that crinkled at the corners of his eyes or the hint of gray mingled with the dark hair at his temples. He was leaner than she remembered, the years having honed his strength to steely precision.

Other things had changed about him, too. The heavy helm he carried under one arm was richly decorated and highly polished. The cloak thrown over his shoulder was fur-lined with an exotic pelt she did not recognize. Even his boots boasted a finer leather than the well-worn pair from her recollection. Not that she had ever cared about his lack of coin. He'd been thoughtful. Strong. Encouraging of her clever mind.

Sweet, merciful heaven, she had loved him.

"I asked Malcolm to send your escort home," he told her without prelude. Without any nod to the fact they had once been far more than acquaintances. "I will bring you to Domhnaill on the morrow."

She shook her head before she could force words from her mouth.

"You cannot." The thought of spending such time with him—isolated together on a journey through the untamed land—struck a mixture of dread and unwanted, impossible hope inside her. "That cannot be."

She would rather return to exile and be a woman disdained by strangers than a woman disdained by this one man. She had learned she could bear a great deal that life had to offer. Her shoulders were strong, as was her will. But her heart—it developed no such armor.

"It is," he informed her succinctly. "You are not in a position to command me any longer."

And was that a hint of pleasure she spied in the hard line of his mouth? Her heart stuttered in her chest at the memory of sweeter words those lips had once spoken to her. Of a chaste kiss by which she compared all other kisses and found them wanting.

"I require no reminding of my place in the world." She refused to ignore the obvious reversal in roles between them. She had fallen far further than he had risen in the world, though it was obvious he had more means and influence now than when they'd last met. Would her father have been so quick to dismiss Cullen of Blackstone's suit if the knight had arrived at Domhnaill dressed thus? Instead, Cullen asked for her hand after a hunting party where one of her father's friends spied them kissing. Her father had been furious long before the offer for her hand had come.

"Of course." He gave her a clipped nod. "I will see you at dawn. We can be in Domhnaill in less than a sennight if we catch a favorable wind once we reach the sea."

He turned to leave and the impending sense of loss threatened to level her. By the saints, now that she had him so near to her again, she feared even his cold words were better than his absence.

"Wait." She stepped toward him and instantly regretted it as he swung to face her. She was too close to him. Did he think about her past as a fallen woman? Did he imagine she enjoyed being so close to men because of her rumored position as a courtesan?

She stepped back immediately, ill to the core even thinking about that.

"What is it?" he prodded, his voice losing a little of its sharp edge.

"I appreciate the offer of an escort and I do not mean to contradict you. Selfishly, I cannot help but think it will be difficult to ride beside you and not remember how different my life might have been."

She had not humbled herself before any man, even those who had been purposely cruel to her. Yet she found herself baring a piece of her heart to this man, sharing the only regret in life that approached the magnitude of giving up her daughter.

"It is important to fight for what we hold dear," he told her, his pale blue eyes meeting hers in the torchlight.

He chastised her still? She was almost grateful for it, since it would be easier to feel angry with him than to feel guilty for her role in sending him away. She understood now that her silence on the subject had been viewed as compliance by Cullen. Had her father regarded it that way, as well? Perhaps she'd held more sway with him than she knew.

"That's why I need to return to Domhnaill. I will fight for my daughter." She would not allow Leah to be raised by a Culcanon. Cristiana had understood all along that Edwina could not allow the Culcanons to touch her babe.

"Do not speak such things." He pulled her close as he hushed her, one hand wrapping about her wrist while the other covered her lips.

Her heart beat so fast to be near him, she could hardly hear the words he whispered near her ear.

"Leah is safe. I was there at Christmas and she looks well. Happy."

She ate up those tidbits he offered, the simple details providing long-needed nourishment for her soul. Each morsel made her happy and hurt her at the same time, given that she had not been able to care for her wee one.

"How did you know she was mine?" She kept her voice low, unsure who they lowered their voices for, since the back hall appeared deserted.

His touch penetrated her sleeve, the warmth of his hand a delight she thought she would never feel again. Even though he did not touch her sweetly, neither did he touch her harshly. For her, it was an unexpected pleasure.

"I guessed when you refused Donegal and your

father packed you off to King William's court nine and a half moons later."

He was a perceptive man. One of many things she'd loved about him. But did he believe her version of events with Donegal, or had he sided with the Culcanons? He'd heard enough of her side from her plea to Malcolm for justice. And no doubt, he'd heard far more about the matter before today.

"Why should I not fight for her then, now that I am finally free to raise her?"

"Because she is happy and safe. Cristiana is the only mother she has ever known and now Duncan the Brave of Culcanon has claimed the girl as his."

Righteous indignation simmered in her veins, overriding any pleasure in standing beside Cullen.

"And what will happen when Duncan makes peace with his maggot-faced half brother? He could hand her over to her rightful father, and I will die before I let that happen." Years' worth of anger spilled into her words. She trembled at the very thought.

Although she hadn't been able to raise Leah, she would protect her wherever she could. Always. Edwina was intensely grateful to Cristiana for raising her daughter—a burden that had surely been as heavy and isolating in its own way as Edwina's exile had been. But how could Cristiana expose the child to such danger now?

Cullen studied her intently, his gaze curious even

though his hand fell away from her arm. His powerful chest expanded with a sigh.

"Time has not dulled your spirit," he pronounced finally. "Welcome home, Edwina."

Her heartbeat faltered. No man should have such power over a woman.

"Time has taught me patience." And bitterness. And regret. But she would not reveal all to this knight. What if he'd taken a wife? What if he did not recall the feelings he'd once had for her? "I am willing to fight for what I want and what I am due."

At last, the mask of dispassion cracked and Cullen of Blackstone grinned. In that moment, he was ageless, the same man she remembered from her youth.

"Fighting has long been a strength of yours." He bowed—bowed!—to her, the quick duck of his head not exactly respectful, but definitely a kindness her now station no longer warranted. "I will look forward to accompanying you on the journey home."

Hope stirred again, that foolish, foolish emotion she had no business feeling. It was sure to do her in.

"Thank you. I know Malcolm has given Domhnaill and any of my inheritance to Duncan, but I still have hope of finding a place with my sister." She did not mention she planned to be sure wedding vows never took place between her sister and Culcanon. And if they already had, Edwina would surmount that obstacle when she came to it.

Cullen frowned a moment before voices from the

hall grew louder. Men approached their corridor. Seizing her again, Cullen placed a hand about her waist and guided her into a nook she thought was another hall but as her knee hit a wooden rim of some sort, she realized they had ducked into the well shaft positioned at the outer corner of a tower. A stairwell loomed above and below them while buckets lined the floor of the shaft for easy access to water.

But then her confusion dispersed when Cullen's hand lingered on her hip, his body pressed close so he could speak quietly in her ear.

"Shh," he warned, his warm breath a caress through her hair that would have sent her into a swoon if she thought she could do so quietly.

Vaguely, she wondered why he sought to hide his presence. Did he not wish to be spotted with her? The thought hurt enough to dull her pleasure in his nearness. Then her disappointment was chased away by Henry's voice on the other side of the thick timber wall.

"She loves another anyhow," Henry confided dully to whomever he walked with. "She only used me to return to Scotland, but she says her heart is for another."

Her eyes widened. There could be no mistaking the voice. Even Cullen would recognize that Norman accent since the keep was full of Scots. Their footsteps receded, leaving their world quiet except for the distant murmur of water deep within the well below.

Her eyes went to Cullen's in the shadowed darkness lit only by a shaft of moonlight through an exterior window and a bit of reflected torchlight from the corridor outside the open door.

Would he guess who she cared for? His pale eyes remained inscrutable while his heart hammered her chest.

She opened her mouth to speak—whether to confess or deny the truth, she did not know, for Cullen spoke first.

"Malcolm did not give Domhnaill to Duncan."

It took her a moment to recall their conversation. She'd been so rattled by Henry's revelation of her feelings for Cullen.

When she retraced their talk, everything inside her stilled. All thoughts of indulging her own feelings died.

"He did not?" She thought back to Cristiana's letter. There could be no mistaking her sister's belief that the keep had gone to Duncan by royal decree. "Then he told a falsehood of mammoth proportions to my family."

And he'd given her a way to ensure a marriage was not valid if arranged under false pretense. Cristiana had more reason than ever to break a betrothal to him.

"I do not know what happened, but I have been

at Malcolm's side long enough to know he endorsed Duncan's rule at Domhnaill, but he would have considered other strong knights if they had the might and means to safeguard those lands."

Betrayal echoed through her as dark and bottomless as the well. A Culcanon had played them false once again.

She looked up entreatingly at him as she gripped the front of his tunic.

"We must hurry to Domhnaill with all haste." Her objective clear, she was spurred to action. "We have a wedding to stop."

Chapter Thirteen

"Mother, I am a real warrior now," Leah called from her perch on Duncan's lap, waving a sword fashioned of two flat pieces of wood strapped together with the leather tie from Duncan's saddlebag.

They lingered beside a shallow creek just beyond the Culcanon town walls, where Duncan had treated them to a ride through freshly fallen snow to give them an outing and some fresh air. They'd paused beside the frozen creek bank so Leah could slide and play on the ice. Now Duncan amused her while he sat on an old, dead log, making toy weapons of war.

"You are fearsome indeed," Cristiana called back, surprised to recognize the warm feeling in her chest.

Happiness. Contentment.

Some few, precious days had passed since the

night Cristiana confessed her attraction to Duncan. By night, he came to her and touched her, inspiring seemingly limitless passion. She caught herself daydreaming about their nights during the day, her wayward thoughts bringing hot color to her cheeks at the most inappropriate times.

Duncan had asked her to take a step toward building trust between them and she had done so. In truth, he had not asked her for anything she did not gladly provide. Lying beside him when darkness fell was a pleasure matched only by moments like this when she watched him charm Leah, patiently demonstrating how to wield her sturdy blade of tree bark.

"She need not fear bad men now." Duncan picked up Leah and spun her around before returning to the horses for their return to the keep. "What knave would dare to approach a maid so fierce?"

Duncan sat Leah on his saddle before throwing his own leg over the beast's back. Cristiana had already mounted, her fingers numb from lingering in winter's chill.

She appreciated Duncan's reassuring words and hoped they were true. Leah had not slept well in the days that followed their trip to Culcanon, frequently dreaming of bad men coming for them. Perhaps the sight of her wooden sword beside her pallet each night would help her feel safe.

"Thank you." Cristiana mouthed the words to

him over Leah's head as they turned their horses around.

"She will be fine," he returned softly, mindful of the child's ears as she stroked his horse's mane with the side of her new toy. "It is not in her nature to be fearful. She will rest well if she believes in her own strength."

"You have been so good to her." Cristiana wondered if he understood how much the girl already admired and cared for him. Affection could swell so quickly when unchecked by the wisdom of age.

Or was it the cynicism of advancing age?

Cristiana envied the carefree joy of child-like love even as she recalled how much it hurt to have those feelings betrayed.

"Not nearly as sweet as she has been to me," Duncan argued, his voice quiet as he rode close enough to her that their legs brushed against each other now and then. "'Tis humbling to know a child's love."

His thoughts were so aligned with hers she wondered how they ever disagreed to the point where they needed to dissolve their relationship completely. She studied him in the pale sunlight, his handsome features the sort that would stand the test of time.

"How much longer will we be here?" She had not bothered to ask him about the future since their initial arguments about the marriage. They still had not spoken their vows in front of a priest. "Donegal has not bothered any travelers these last few nights, so there is no one to fight. Besides, if we return to Domhnaill, I can help you find your treasure."

The clomp of the horses' hooves echoed in the frosty air.

"Moving you now could be risky." Duncan's gaze tracked the horizon in a habit she recognized from their journey here. "Donegal does not have many men, so he must resort to scattered attacks to reduce my numbers. He is out there, and he will strike again. I fear for your sister if she truly attempts the trek home now."

Everything within her went still.

"I did not warn her." She'd written to Edwina of all the happenings with Duncan, excited for her sister to return home, but she had not referenced Donegal's recent attacks and thievery. "At the time I didn't even know—"

"She will be escorted." Duncan steered his mount toward the drawbridge leading into Culcanon's second story. Cristiana's followed. "And not many men would risk travel up the east coast in winter. Edwina may have no choice but to wait until spring."

Cristiana tried to picture her sister biding her time patiently until the thaw, and could not. In the few letters they had exchanged over the years, Edwina had seemed as bold as ever—the same untamed spirit as Leah, honed with a woman's strength.

No doubt, Edwina made her way toward Domhnaill

even as Donegal ran roughshod over unsuspecting travelers. What would he do if he happened upon her on a deserted forest road?

The horses' hooves echoed hollowly on the drawbridge, the sound vibrating dully through her.

"Edwina will not wait." She looked to Duncan, realizing how much she had come to rely on him already. Away from her home and her people, she had little choice, of course. But Duncan had more than earned her faith in his sword arm and his ability to protect her. "I pray you are almost ready to seek out your brother and bring an end to his crimes."

As they reached the courtyard, Leah's nurse approached, a young maid who had followed them to Culcanon with their trunks a few days after their arrival. She reached up to take the child, though she frowned in worry at the sight of Leah's new toy.

Duncan did not answer her until the little girl had been whisked away for a morsel in the kitchen. Only then did he swing down off his horse and move to help Cristiana to the ground.

"I had hoped to gather more men. Building protective forces for two keeps requires many blades and assembling a riding party strong enough to hunt an outlaw means we need still more." His hands fit securely around her waist, the warmth of his touch far more decadent than her layers of rich fabrics, heating her skin in contrast to the words that chilled her insides with fear. "But if you truly think Edwina rides this way—"

"I do." She leaned into his strength, trusting him in this regard. "I would stake my life upon it."

He lowered her slowly, allowing her soft curves to graze the hard surface of his chain-mail-covered chest. Her breath caught in spite of herself, in spite of the seriousness of their discussion. The horses and men, hay carts and wood bearers, all faded away in the courtyard.

"I would not have you stake your life on a simple wager, wife."

Her heart sped at the heated look in his eyes. He brushed over her lips. A light, passing graze of his mouth, but it was more than he'd ever claimed from her in public.

"Very well." He released her as she realized her feet now touched the hard-packed earth. "I will assemble men to take on the task. We will leave at dawn to rid the roads of this scourge."

Like a balm to her soul, the vow wound around her as securely as his arms had moments ago. With effort on both sides, they were rebuilding trust between them, just as he'd said they would.

Trust would not come overnight, but perhaps with time, it would yet return.

"Thank you." Gratitude filled her, chasing away the chill from the winter air. "I will notify the kitchen and help with preparations—"

A shout went up from the tower gatehouse at the same time a horn sounded nearby.

The whole courtyard stilled except for Duncan. The laird vaulted back onto his horse and raced toward the tower, where a watch stood guard over the bridge.

Knowing the alert could not possibly bode well, Cristiana followed him. She threw herself on her horse's back as no groom had led the mount away yet. Riding clumsily toward the tower gate, she thanked the saints Leah was already inside the keep. On trembling legs, she slid from her horse and climbed the stairs to the battlements, desperate to know what danger approached. She reached Duncan's side in time to see a riding party closing in fast. The horses ran full out over the surrounding hill, their riders leaning deep over their mounts to urge the most speed possible.

"Do they not see the moat?" Cristiana could not fathom their purpose. The riders were too small in number to mount an attack. Why ride so fiercely for the gates? "If we raise the bridge, the first line is sure to perish in the fall."

The guard in charge of the bridge mechanism looked expectantly at Duncan, awaiting a command.

"Leave it," he ordered, his eyes still on the field and the oncoming riders.

Cristiana wanted to argue, having recently discovered how easily a keep could be taken by stealth when a conqueror disguised himself as a traveler seeking shelter. But first her eye caught sight of a pale swath of fabric beneath a wind-tossed cloak. Narrowing her gaze, she had the impression that this particular rider wore a surcoat beneath a dark cape.

"It seems we will not have to return to Domhnaill after all," Duncan announced, turning away from the battlements. "I believe your sister has arrived."

Dark foreboding arrived along with Lady Edwina of Domhnaill.

Duncan could feel the change in the air despite the squeal of high-pitched female greetings and the wealth of happy tears. His ability to read people and moods had made him a good diplomat for Malcolm abroad, and he could see the latent thirst for vengeance in Edwina's eyes the moment she galloped into his courtyard and swung down at Cristiana's feet, sweeping her sister into a hug.

If only Duncan had cultivated his talent before his trip to the continent. He might have seen Donegal's perfidy and the Domhnaills' honesty long ago. But then, perhaps his ordeal with these people had helped him refine his skills in the first place.

Now, while the women clutched each other and exchanged whispered words in the hall, Cullen of Blackstone confided the details of their journey to Duncan.

"We were set upon by thieves just outside Domhnaill's

gates." Cullen gulped mead and broth while servers hastened to find more substantial food for the guests. "I lost three good men and sent back to Domhnaill for reinforcements."

Duncan had already noted several horses and men with flesh wounds that needed tending. After all of Blackstone's riders were within the walls, he'd ordered the gates closed. Donegal was attacking more frequently, acquiring good horseflesh and weapons for each kill.

And Duncan planned to take an inventory of everything Donegal had stolen to help sharpen his knowledge of the enemy. For too long he'd allowed the bonds of kinship to blind him regarding his half brother. But first, he had more immediate concerns for the newcomer swilling mead like a man dying of thirst.

"Why did you come?" Duncan did not care if the query sounded inhospitable.

Cullen replaced his drinking horn on the table, not quite hiding his surprise at the question.

"Edwina has been parted from her sister for too many summers." The older knight's gaze went to the seat at the dais where the women had the run of the table. Cristiana served Edwina herself, calling for furs and blankets while she spooned broth into her sister's mouth. "If you'd seen how close the two of them were during their growing-up years—"

Duncan's fist hit the table. He could not stomach

Blackstone's eyes on Cristiana for even one more moment.

"You expect me to believe you brought danger to my door in the heart of winter for the sake of a woman's wants?" He edged into the knight's space, ready to make his message clear. "I know exactly why you are here. But you will never touch Cristiana as long as I draw breath."

Blackstone did a credible job of feigning surprise. Confusion.

"I have never coveted Lady Cristiana—"

"Then why did she think you would wed her to keep Domhnaill out of my hands?" He could not bear the thought of this man under his roof, knowing Cristiana would have given herself to him to avoid marriage to Duncan.

Again, Blackstone appeared caught unawares. He set down his broth and shook his head.

"I had no idea she hatched such a scheme, but I can only think she felt safe with me because I once loved her sister. I offered for Edwina before—Donegal." The bitterness on the man's tongue could not have been more apparent. This distaste was no act.

The pieces shifted into place, making sense. Cristiana had not sought a marriage to Cullen because she found him pleasing. She had sought him out because she felt secure with him.

Around Duncan, the noise of Blackstone's knights warming themselves with fine mead faded. His glance

stole to Cristiana again, her expression worried as
Edwina spoke earnestly in her ear. He hoped her sibling had not brought more bad news. Duncan would
have his hands full flushing out Donegal and all his
followers. Between the crimes of his brother, two
keeps to manage and Culcanon's empty coffers, he
had enough obstacles to surmount. He did not need
any more trouble.

"I see." He believed the man. But that belief did not
make it any easier to have him under his roof when
Cristiana had considered giving her innocence to him.
"Would a fat dowry be enough enticement for you to
resume your pursuit of Edwina?"

The sooner he could settle the sister away from
here, the less attention she would draw to his household. If Donegal knew Edwina had returned, he might
increase his efforts to claim the keep. Claim Leah.

And that, Duncan could not have. Sooner or later,
Donegal would suspect he had fathered the girl. Would
he use the child as a means to rally more supporters?
Some men might believe he had been wronged by
Edwina and lend their swords to a movement to take
back the child. Duncan had not only vowed to protect
Leah, he had come to care for the bold little lass a
great deal. He would allow no harm to come to her.

Perhaps if Edwina was far away, wed and protected by a strong knight, Donegal would not give
her another thought.

"I am not sure." Cullen's gaze had returned to the

women. And, Duncan now acknowledged, it was Edwina who claimed the older knight's interest.

Cristiana's elder sister still spoke fervently, her hands in motion to emphasize her words. Cristiana's once-joyous expression had shifted to a dark frown. Her eyes studied a spot on the table, as if all her thoughts were focused on what she heard and not what she saw.

Then, as if she'd felt his stare, she looked up. Their eyes locked and he expected to feel that warm, growing connection that had developed between them recently.

Instead, he felt the sharp daggers of her displeasure evident in her gaze. Hastily, she looked back down to the table, but he had not mistaken what he'd seen. Edwina had apparently returned with news that did not please her sister. And somehow *he* had become a source of unhappiness.

Turning his attention back to his guest, his sense of foreboding increased.

"Consider the arrangement this eve and give me an answer in the morn." He rose, more determined than ever to confront the brother who continued to betray his family. "One way or another, I will need to wed her off. And soon."

"You are mistaken."

Cristiana trembled inside despite the hearth embers warm on her back. She prayed her unease did not show in her voice. Her sister had endured hardship and hurt beyond anything she could imagine. Cristiana did not wish to appear weakhearted in this matter. She watched Duncan rise and depart the hall, his expression grim.

They had been so close on their ride with Leah earlier this day. Cristiana had felt happy. Hopeful.

"Nay. There is no mistake." Edwina shook her head, her red-gold curls longer than ever in the blossom of womanhood. Her clothing was simple, humble even, despite the position she'd been in at court. But her eyes did not mirror her dress. She might have left Domhnaill a fallen woman, but she returned strong and proud.

"But I was there when we heard there was a messenger from the king." Cristiana had known Duncan to be a favorite of Malcolm's and witnessed the receipt of a communication from the king's own herald. "If Malcolm did not write to give Duncan command of Domhnaill, what could he have wanted?"

"Who knows what business takes up men's time?" Edwina waved the matter away impatiently. "But I was with the king less than a sennight ago and Cullen was in residence there before I arrived. Malcolm did not give away our keep to a Culcanon. Duncan only told Father as much to meet his own ends."

Cristiana recalled the way Duncan had compelled her to open her gates, playing upon her sympathies. Then he'd found a way to stay under her roof with his story of treasure hunting told as an entertainment for her hall. Now, even his basis for wedding her was—it appeared—a lie.

A hole opened within her. Dark and cavernous, the empty space yawned wide on a day that should have been filled with celebrating her sister's return.

Could she have been foolish enough to care for Duncan again after knowing how he'd betrayed her trust the first time? Her aching heart already knew the answer.

To protect herself from the dark wretchedness of that hurt, she called up all the fury that was her right. She'd been lied to. Cheated. Robbed of her sovereignty in her own household.

"Cristiana?" Edwina studied her thoughtfully, as if Cristiana had been the one to make a dangerous journey through the snow and bands of outlaws. "If it is not too much trouble, I would like to see my daughter."

My daughter.

Abruptly, she was yanked from one pain to another. She had dared not even think about this request since her sister had arrived because the thought of losing Leah was unbearable.

She had to close her eyes for a moment while the hurt washed over her. Duncan did not care for her. He wanted what he'd always wanted—Domhnaill. And now, it seemed, Edwina wanted Leah. The possibility of losing her family stabbed through her.

"Those are dangerous words," she warned. "I have protected Leah as my own because you made her thus at her birth."

Edwina nodded, chastened. "Of course, but—"

"No. Her safety is too important for us to make careless mistakes." Cristiana understood her sister's request even when it pained her to have Edwina call Leah "her" daughter. By the laws of nature, it was the truth, obviously. But to a heart already ripped raw, the small slight cut deep. No one would take her daughter away from her. "She is with her nurse, but I will take you to her when you are finished eating."

Edwina dropped her knife and dipped her hands in a bowl of water to the side of the trencher.

"I am done." She dried her hands quickly and stood.

And though years had passed since she left, Cristiana felt the same pull of forces between them. Both of them were strong willed, yet Edwina had always pushed for her way a bit harder.

Not this time.

Cristiana rose more slowly, reeling in too many directions at once. Her world was falling apart like a castle gate beneath a battering ram. The blows just kept coming, and her life kept crumbling away beneath the force. If she was back at home, she would take solace in the mead house where she could at least have control over the brewing, simmering concoctions. Here, she had nothing to distract her from Duncan's betrayal and her sister's return.

And while she would fight Edwina with everything she had, Cristiana didn't think anything could save her from an impending marriage based on lies.

Chapter Fourteen

Duncan knocked on the door to the solar outside Cristiana's bedchamber.

Normally, she slept in his bed, but since her sister had arrived she had remained in Edwina's rooms.

"Who is it?" Her voice was cold and distant. Or was it his imagination?

"Duncan." He opened the door a bit, enough to see that Edwina was not with her, but that the door to the sleeping chamber at the far end of the solar was closed.

"She has fallen asleep," Cristiana explained from her seat near the closed door, apparently keeping watch over her sibling this night instead of joining him in his rooms.

He hated to disturb Cristiana after being parted from her sister for so long, but this could not wait.

He needed to share his new concerns with Cristiana, something he found himself doing more and more since they'd come to Culcanon.

She was more than just his bed partner. More than a sweetly affectionate mother to the daughter he'd claimed as his own. Cristiana was as sharp and insightful about running a household as she was about mead-making. Managing Domhnaill for so many years after her father's health had deteriorated left her with a keen understanding of battle and defense, strategy and alliances.

"There is trouble afoot." He'd been restless for hours, for reasons he could not quite name.

"What do you mean?" She peered up at him from her seat at a heavy, claw-footed table. Shadows loomed under her eyes and he recalled how unhappy she'd appeared while they'd fed their guests earlier. "Trouble with Donegal? Or within the walls at Culcanon?"

He shrugged, unsure how to define his concerns.

"Both, perhaps. I thought to engage Donegal more easily once we came to Culcanon, but now I wonder if he hoped to draw me back here on purpose. Perhaps our move to Culcanon was a mistake from the start." He knew something wasn't right tonight.

Something had bothered him ever since Cullen and Edwina had arrived with a few of Cullen's retainers and men-at-arms borrowed from Domhnaill. They'd only been at that keep briefly, just long enough to find out that Duncan and Cristiana had moved on.

Then they'd gathered up additional men and made the shorter trek to Culcanon so the sisters could be reunited. Or, perhaps, so Edwina could be reunited with the daughter she'd hardly seen since giving birth. Having Edwina around Leah would make him uneasy until he was certain she had no plans to stake a claim to the child.

"It is always humiliating to discover you were wrong." The bite in her words reminded him of the dark looks she'd given him in the great hall.

Had she learned something of his deceits? Or had her sister merely stirred trouble with her old grievances against his family? Either scenario would create difficulty for him.

For them.

"You are angry." Regret fired through him. He'd hoped to find some haven here from the threat his half brother posed. Even with all of Domhnaill at his disposal, he might not have enough to defend two keeps, since Donegal had emptied the weapons stores along with everything else he'd taken.

But instead of finding a moment's retreat from the coming dangers, he found Cristiana had somehow become his enemy, too.

Facing him, her gray eyes narrowed.

"You told me the king awarded you Domhnaill."

She knew. He'd promised himself he would explain

it to her after her heart had softened, but he'd seen no sign of that until earlier today at the river's edge. And then, he'd selfishly soaked up that rare happiness, deceiving himself in thinking he could wait a bit longer.

"I would have told you." He reached for her. "Soon."

She wrenched away.

"Perhaps so. Did you hope to wait until after it didn't matter anymore? After I was already married to you and powerless to change our fate?" The resentment in her rising voice made him recall the way she'd hardened her heart to him five years ago.

She'd become his enemy once when she'd perceived deception on his part, and it had not even been true. How might she grow to hate him now when his trickery had been carefully planned?

"I sought to protect you and your lands."

"You sought to recover the keep you lost when I broke our betrothal! Do not pretend an altruism you did not feel. I am not so naive as that, Duncan. Not anymore." Her stare was cold. A veil had fallen between them, closing him out of the more tender emotions he'd seen in her these past days.

"I could have demanded justice for that broken betrothal." His father had urged him to, but he had not wished to pursue a woman so intent on hating him. "It was within my right."

"So instead of demanding the marriage then,

you waited until you really needed Domhnaill, and demanded it later? By deceit, no less?" Her voice broke and she turned from him, her arms wrapped tightly about herself. "Do not speak to me of your rights."

He'd hurt her. At some point, early on in all of this when he'd first stood at her doorstep, he probably intended to. But somewhere along the way, he'd come to care about her more than he'd ever intended. More than he'd wanted.

And the hurt he spied within her speared him as well.

"I am sorry." Sorry for what might have been between them. Sorry for many things.

He was not surprised that she made no response.

"Cristiana, perhaps our fate was decided five years ago, after a kiss so powerful neither of us have ever forgotten it." He meant that. He'd been running away from that truth for too long. "I went halfway around the world to put you out of my mind and I couldn't. Perhaps it's time you admit how much of a hold the past has had over you, too. Think about that next time you're brewing mead on the very spot where we promised to be together for all time."

"You lied to me again!" She raised her voice, seemingly heedless of her sister sleeping in the adjoining chamber. "We were supposed to be building back trust, but all along you knew we built nothing on a foundation of deceit."

The unshed tears in her eyes shredded his insides like an enemy blade. But by the rood, he'd had noble intentions mixed up with all the rest.

"If you had seen the devastations of battle that I have, you would appreciate the humanity of a blood-less takeover." He did not want to think about how vulnerable Cristiana and her old father had been before he arrived. "Do you have any idea how easily Domhnaill could have fallen into far more malicious hands than mine? The whole of Scotland knew of your father's infirmities since he hasn't shown his face in Malcolm's court for years. Your keep was ripe for taking."

"And you had to be the man to benefit from our misfortune? It wasn't enough for you that your family twisted a knife in our backs once before? You would not let us rest until you claimed all the same wealth you sought five years ago."

He told himself it was just as well she thought he'd been gold hunting from the start. His pride would only suffer along with the rest of him if she knew how she'd conquered far more with a simple kiss than he'd managed in all this time.

"You are healthy and safe from harm, as is our daughter. As is your father. In a time of unrest when a laird fails in his duties as your father neglected his for too long, that is a great deal to be thankful for. And even if you are not, *I* am thankful that you have not known more misfortune in this shift of power, though I truly regret you feel misused."

Unsure how else to explain himself when she was ready to believe the worst of him—still—he turned on his heel to leave.

"I am thankful for all of those things." Her voice was so soft he feared he would see tears in her eyes if he confronted her now, and *that* he could not bear. Not when his grip on his own emotions was tenuous at best.

"I do not expect thanks—" He started.

"But how am I to feel when you have deceived me at every turn? You could have arrived at my keep to request a meeting with the laird. Instead you request-ed shelter to entreat me to open the gates, all the while planning to betray me once you were within the walls—"

Within the walls. The words unlocked a puzzle that had been rattling around his head.

"Hellfire." At once, he understood what had been niggling at his brain ever since Edwina and Cullen had arrived. They'd come with a mix of retainers and men-at-arms not well known to one another. They'd fought a battle and lost men en route.

What if some of their attackers secretly joined the travelling party? What if traitors even now slept in his keep? Or worse, opened the gates to still more while they slept?

"What is it?" Cristiana's face paled, perhaps

reading some of the gut-wrenching fear that just twisted around his innards.

Edwina stumbled sleepily into the chamber, a blanket around her shoulders like a cape, her red-gold hair a mirror image of her sister's.

"What is it?" she mumbled, peering from Cristiana to Duncan and back again.

"I think our defenses have been breached. Invaders could have entered with Edwina unbeknownst to her." He hauled open the door to the corridor and sprinted down the hall, shouting as he left. "Find Leah. Lock yourselves in the keep and do not emerge from there unless I come for you."

Cristiana tore down a winding set of steps and then up another, following the convoluted path to the children's sleeping chamber. Was she going in the correct direction? Panic had robbed her of rational thought, her maternal heart rattling her whole body with every erratic beat.

Her chest burned as she panted for air. The way to the chamber was purposefully confusing, intended to shield the occupants from just the kind of attack Duncan was afraid had happened—enemies lurking inside the walls. But the hidden passages would present no problem to Donegal's men, many of whom had once called this keep home before defecting to the side of the traitor.

"Cristiana?" Edwina's voice carried through the darkness from somewhere behind her.

"Up here." Cristiana held a hand to her heart, thinking if she could slow the frantic beat, maybe her thoughts would clear. "There is a narrow staircase that veers off to the left of the main steps."

She could picture where her sister had grown confused. Why couldn't she remember the way from here? The trek through the dark had taken only moments, but it felt like hours when she wasn't sure if Leah would be safe at the other end. It was like a dream where nameless terrors chased her and she could never find her way out of a dim maze.

The remembered corridors of Domhnaill overlapped with the less-familiar floor plan of Culcanon, a sea of maps and directions blurring when she needed to find her way to her little girl.

She heard Edwina approach, but did not look up, her mind on the verge of remembering a route she'd travelled several times but forgot in a haze of fear. All at once, her cloudy thoughts crystallized, growing sharp once again. The halls and passages of Culcanon and Domhnaill became distinct, her thoughts focused. Oddly, she only remembered where Leah slept during her brain's fitful seizure.

While she struggled to unlink the overlapping keeps in her mind, she also suddenly realized where the treasure must have been hidden from the Norsemen back at Domhnaill.

"This way." She grabbed Edwina's hand and pulled her up the rest of the steps, desperate to see Leah. She had never known such helpless fear.

"I will never forgive myself if I endangered Leah by coming here." Edwina's strangled sob echoed all the fear Cristiana felt inside. "I was so intent on revenge when I should have been grateful my daughter—*your* daughter—was safe."

Turning a sharp corner and finding a door to yet another staircase, Cristiana led her sister up it.

"A mother's heart always finds a way to feel guilt." Cristiana knew this all too well. "We blame ourselves if a child sneezes or speaks inappropriately at the table or tumbles down a hill. If Leah is not there, I will say it is my fault for ever allowing Duncan to keep us here. Or for not bringing her in my chamber every night—"

"Mother?"

The small, sweet voice of her daughter bounced through the halls to Cristina's ears. She nearly sank to the cold stone floor with relief.

"Leah!" She hadn't realized she could run even faster, yet somehow she did. "My angel." Spotting the girl's face peeking out from the large chamber door, Cristiana raced to close the distance between them. "You are well."

She wrapped the girl in her arms, squeezing, kissing, hugging. Edwina did the same, squeezing, kissing and hugging both of them. Edwina had introduced herself to the child as her "aunt," and Leah had taken to her immediately. It was wrong of Cristiana to feel any envy of her sister after what Edwina had gone through, but she could not help the occasional twinges, knowing Edwina's bond with Leah was an unbreakable blood tie. For now, Cristiana was merely grateful they were all safe.

"I heard your voices in the hall," Leah told them, brushing her hair from her eyes. "The sounds echo and make it hard to sleep. There have been so many footsteps."

Slowly, the child's words filtered through her relief. She'd heard the sound of someone walking outside the corridors? Enough to wake her from her bed to see what happened outside her chamber?

Unease closed a cold fist about her gut.

"Footsteps?" She released Leah at the same time as Edwina, puzzling over that comment. Some of the footfall sounds would have been hers and Edwina's. But their slippers were far quieter than the echo of a man's heavy boot.

"Do not move." A deep, masculine voice filled the corridor just as Leah let out a scream.

Cristiana reached for her, but the child was yanked back forcefully out of her reach. A man-at-arms thick as a pillar held a blade to Leah's delicate neck, the silver glinting dully in the inky darkness broken only by the glow of the hearth from inside the children's sleeping chamber.

Edwina clutched Cristiana's arm, her fingers like talons in her skin. The sister, who had once been afraid of nothing, was more terrified than Cristiana had ever seen her. Yet she could not possibly feel half the fear Cristiana did.

Do not let him hurt her, she prayed.

"She is only a child," Cristiana warned, wondering if the man possessed a soul to touch such a helpless creature. "There are more lucrative hostages—"

"There's only one that will do for my lord." The man kept Leah pressed tightly to his side, his splayed palm the size of her small back. "As the first heir to Culcanon, she will help us claim what is rightfully his."

They knew. Somehow, Donegal and his men had learned of Leah's existence. The truth she'd kept hidden so carefully was a secret no more.

"Donegal will skewer you if you harm this child." Edwina's threat sounded vicious despite the tearful gasp that escaped at the end of it.

"That is why I hope you will be smart enough to stand back and let me take her." The brigard brandished the blade toward them, making them jump back a step.

Leah yelped, a small, helpless sound that tugged at Cristiana's heart. Then, quicker than a blink, the invader disappeared down another passage—a corridor Cristiana did not recognize.

"Do not worry, Leah," Cristiana called out blindly,

counting on the echoing stone to carry the message to her daughter. "Your papa will come for you."

And he would. While Edwina alerted the maids and other children still in the chamber behind them, Cristiana hastened down the stairwell to find Duncan. He would save Leah.

Hadn't he risked his life before to save her? He would do so again. This much she knew. In fact, as she ran past the timber reinforcements and doorways toward the main keep, Cristiana was overwhelmed by her own certainty, a faith in Duncan in at least this much.

And wasn't that what mattered most? That he kept her daughter safe? Of all the times to realize nothing else mattered…

But if she thought about it, she would have to admit that every way he'd deceived her had been his way of keeping her safe—and later, Leah, as well. He'd warned Cristiana that a takeover could be bloody, and that his manipulation had been better because no lives had been lost. But she could not see past her pride to the truth of that until someone invaded her home and dragged her child from her bed to help a scum-sucking wretch in his grasp for power.

She'd been a fool to question Duncan's bid for Domhnaill, when he had harmed no one. When she had let years lapse without urging her father to find a replacement to rule.

She only hoped it wasn't too late to tell him she

had been blind. Prideful and stubborn. But first, she had to let him know that Leah was in terrible, terrible danger.

Chapter Fifteen

Duncan was halfway to his horse when he stopped himself.

And thought.

He'd planned to leave Culcanon's walls to engage this brigand army of rebels that plagued his people— to call out his rogue brother and meet him with his sword. But with the still, cold air of winter blowing around him, his passions cooled and reason reined again.

He'd planned to leave Cullen behind in charge of the women and ferreting out anyone who'd sneaked into the keep with his party. For his part, Duncan would lead a charge to flush the outlaws from the forest and rid his lands of his brother's dangerous ambition.

But why resort to the sword now when he'd

accomplished so much through shrewdness and diplomacy? Hadn't he travelled the continent for the king all those years to learn skills that spared lives and left towns in tact?

"We have unfinished business here," he called to his second in command—a younger knight, since he'd left Rory in charge of Domhnaill. "Spread out and man the walls on the ground. A traitor seeks to breach our defenses tonight and we must be ready to stop the scourge where it flows."

Confusion followed his announcement. There was muttering among the men as the horses stomped impatiently in the cold. But his second in command barked out orders on top of the questions and grumbles, orchestrating a mass movement of their limited resources.

He was almost back to the keep when Cristiana ran out the main doors, Cullen close behind her. By the deathly pallor of her skin, he feared he already knew what she would say.

"They've taken Leah." Her voice shook, but not half as much as her hand as she latched on to his arm and squeezed. "A man I did not recognize held her at the point of his blade and said he would take her to his overlord. I can only assume he means Donegal."

Rage rumbled up out of his gut and spewed through his blood like a poison. The need to lift his own sword to avenge anyone threatening that precious girl—his girl—was so potent he almost forgot his cursed plan to wield words before steel.

"Duncan, please." Cristiana's urgent voice called him back from the darkness. "He disappeared down a side hall near the children's chamber. I did not dare to follow them for fear he would hurt her—"

"Of course." He had not thought of it before, but then he did not consider anyone who remained in the village would be loyal to Donegal after the way his half brother had run the lands into the ground and robbed the keep of any wealth he could move. "There is a passage to the outskirts of the town, but still within the walls."

His fury still simmered to think of a man with a sword standing so close to Cristiana and daring to touch his daughter. The light, falling snow did not begin to soothe the hot anger churning within, but it did remind him that Leah faced another danger in her captor's hands. A child could freeze in no time at all being dragged around through this kind of weather.

He turned to Cullen. "Ask one of the servers to show you the staircase near the children's chamber that leads to the village. It must be barred up and guarded immediately."

The man nodded and left, his unquestioning haste to do Duncan's bidding chasing any remaining doubts he might have had about the Blackstone knight from his mind.

He wrapped an arm about Cristiana, a plan

forming. As much as he wanted to wreak unholy vengeance on anyone who would wield a weapon at a child, he was more certain than ever he needed to trap the treacherous within the walls before he could stomp out the brigands outside.

"You think we can surprise them at the other end?" She hastened her step. "I can take Leah and you can throw that pig of a man into the dungeon until he rots."

Here was the woman who had spent her youth hunting alongside her father. She was strong. Ready to fight. What would their marriage have been like if she'd been willing to fight for him?

"No." Reaching the outer wall of the keep, he steered her toward the stairs leading up to the ramparts. "We will put our people to work and help them reclaim their homes and their safety."

"What about Leah?" She maintained his fast pace, even though he suspected she'd far rather run to the end of the keep's escape route in hopes of saving the girl herself.

"This will bring her back," he assured her, finally seeing the way to unseat Donegal for good.

As they reached the top and broke out into the sunlight again, Duncan called to the herald and asked for all the townspeople to be brought together in the courtyard. His men would remain on watch around the perimeter of the town's walls, but everyone else began to assemble as soon as the herald brought his horn to his lips. From all around Culcanon, maids and churls, tradesmen and farmers who worked his land departed their homes and gathered in the courtyard.

No doubt they responded all the more quickly, since the whole town knew of the recent unrest. The riding party Duncan had called and then dismissed earlier had roused much interest.

"You will speak to them?" Cristiana worried her lip with her teeth, peering over the ramparts as if she expected the villagers to begin launching arrows their way any moment.

"You already know I will protect Leah with my sword and my life." He tugged her back from the wall, placing her by his side, where he would address the throng. "Trust me when I tell you this is a more potent strength."

She looked disbelieving, and he supposed he should be flattered her faith in his knightly skill was so great. Mostly, he feared she would never bring herself to trust him again.

Steeling himself to accomplish the task before him and bring Leah home, he turned back to the ramparts and lifted his voice.

"People of Culcanon, it's been too many years since I lived among you." He knew time was of the essence today, but he could not rush his plea. Not when the reward could be so great. "In my work for our king and my efforts to obtain a worthy lady for our lands, I have been away more than I've been here. I tell myself this is why some of you have chosen to support the only leader you've known since my father died, a leader who fouled the lands with his greed, selling off crops to outsiders that could have fed you."

Duncan took stock of the utter quiet in the courtyard. Never had a thousand people been so silent. He could hear his family banner snap in the breeze beside him as he looked out to study the upturned faces below. He scoured the far reaches of the lands with his gaze, hoping to see Leah and her captor hidden among the rest.

"But I tell you now that my half brother has forsaken us. You, me and even the fortress my ancestors built two hundred years ago. Donegal has stripped the keep of every ornament and bauble he could sell to support a rebellion that will never take place. And do you know why that rebellion will not take place?"

He paused, folding his arms upon the battlements for a moment while his people considered the question. Then, leaning back again to stand tall, he continued.

"Because I will not suffer a traitor in my home any more than you will suffer traitors among you."

There was a roll of mutterings and murmurs at this proclamation. Duncan listened to it, satisfied with the ebbs and flows of the crowd's reactions, which he could not have scripted any better. Now all he had to do was incite them to action.

If only he was as skilled at influencing Cristiana.

"We know they are there," he called out over the villagers. "Donegal receives supplies and manpower from somewhere each moonrise. The odds that those supplies come from supporters within Culcanon's walls are overwhelming. So I tell you this today. Anyone supporting my brother has my blessing to pack and leave the gates by nightfall. For families with children, I will even be sure you have enough food for a sennight. But anyone who chooses to remain will renounce all ties to an outlaw and a thief—" he hardened his voice, allowing the fierceness of his anger to come through "—for my half brother has stolen my daughter and sole heir."

By now, the crowd was in such frenzy, he had to raise his hand to call for the herald's horn again.

When quiet reigned—and he knew it would be brief—he made his final request with Cristiana at his side, her veils and her long hair streaking against his back in the wind.

"We can protect our homes and our families from this scourge that bears my blood, but it means we stand united. We will cast out all traitors from our midst and rebuild Culcanon, but only when I receive my daughter back home and unharmed. Anyone who knowingly gives shelter to the man who stole her—or the man who ordered her taken—will feel my wrath."

From beside him, Cristiana nodded with approval.

"They will all search for her." She wrung her hands together, her knuckles white with fear. "And with your men at all the walls, no one will leave the town without them seeing."

He nodded, glad that she had recognized his intentions and realized the potential payoff. With her intelligence and talents alongside his, they could rule a prosperous and thriving domain for many, many years. If only she would give him that chance.

From below, a lone woman's scream diverted his attention. Together with Cristiana, he looked down to the courtyard just as mass chaos erupted.

On the outskirts of town, one crofter's hut billowed black smoke into the sky while the structure beside it sparked into flame.

Somehow, Donegal and his men would escape.

Cristiana feared it with all her soul as she raced into the courtyard behind Duncan. He'd shouted orders the whole way, putting Cullen of Blackstone into action as all the people who'd been locked safely in the keep poured out into the bailey to help contain the fire.

Acrid smoke filled the courtyard, the dried grasses and twigs used for most of the crude shelters catching fire instantly. Where was Leah in all this?

Eyes burning from the flying ash and thick soot, Cristiana blinked as she ran. Panic clogged her throat more than the smoke as she thought about how frightened Leah must be. Ahead of her, she saw Duncan disappear into the thick gray air as if he knew exactly where to go. Had he anticipated his brother's next move? She had no doubt but that Donegal was behind this.

"Cristiana, wait!" From behind her, she heard Edwina's voice.

Unsure where else to run, Cristiana slowed her step as Edwina caught up.

"I lost Duncan. I can't see where I'm going." Around her, people shouted and ran, as if the whole of Culcanon knew what to do. But with people hurrying in so many different directions, it didn't make sense to follow any of them without a plan.

"You will catch fire if you are not careful." Edwina stooped at Cristiana's feet and grabbed the ends of her cloak, tying them together below her hips so the fabric did not fly up as she ran.

Cristiana noticed her sister had already secured her own cloak thus. Oddly, with the clouds of gray surrounding them, her eyes settled upon the one flash of brightness she could see. A hint of silver about her sister's finger.

Instinctively, the clutched Edwina's hand and stared at the band of heavy, hammered silver studded with deep red garnets.

"What is this?" She stumbled forward as someone knocked her in the leg with a bucket of sloshing water. She hardly noticed.

Edwina drew back her fingers and straightened before pulling Cristiana through the smoke.

"Cullen gave it to me this morning." Her voice contained a girlish sweetness and disbelief so unlike her usual bold, adventurous self. "He said he would take the dowry Duncan offered, but only because it is a symbol of my worth and not because he needs it." She squeezed Cristiana's arm harder as her voice broke. "Do you believe him? He says I am worth a treasure, but he will donate the dowry to the church near his keep. I never guessed a person could swing from such happiness to such depths of fear in one simple day."

Cristiana understood completely. Right now, even as she felt relief for her sister's security, fear for Leah swamped all else.

"He is a good man." Privately, she thanked the saints she had never been able to ask Cullen to wed her. All this time, he had still loved Edwina. "You deserve the kind of happy marriage that brought mother and father contentment for so many years."

Finally, they made it through the worst of the smoke to come out on the end of the town where the two cottages had been burning. Villagers had made a human chain to pass buckets of water from the well to the fire, their cooperation evident in the speed with which they'd contained the blaze. Now, soot and ash poured from the simmering, sizzling mess of stinking, charred straw. But flames sparked no more.

"Praise God," Cristiana murmured, relieved that Duncan's tenants had halted the spread of a fire that could have left the whole town homeless in winter.

"Cristiana." Duncan appeared beside her, his face streaked with soot and dirt, his sword in hand. "She is not in the passage from the keep to the village. The townspeople helped me to chase out three men hiding within the hidden tunnel, but Leah was not among them."

Cullen arrived behind him, his expression as somber as Duncan's. Wordlessly, the other man stood behind Edwina. In that moment, Cristiana could see how they fit together—his silent strength and her vibrant determination. Any worries she'd had about her sister returning and possibly reclaiming Leah faded in the face of needing all the strength and resources she could muster to keep the girl safe. No child could have too many protectors.

Chapter Sixteen

"And you're certain no one has escaped the town walls?" Cristiana asked. Her eyes veered away from her sister to the townspeople, who doused nearby cottages in case the flames sparked back to life.

"I know every one of those men personally and can vouch for their trustworthiness," Duncan replied. "They would never allow any man to escape the town once they had orders to keep the perimeter secure."

"My lord?" An older woman had approached them at some point, her cloak singed on one side and her hair tied back in a heavy linen head covering.

Her clothes marked her as someone who worked in the fields during the warm months. She carried an infant in her arms and she bent low with the babe once she had Duncan's attention.

"Aye?" His tone was polite enough, though Cristiana saw the impatience in his eyes.

How had she come to know him and his moods so well? She surely hadn't been able to clearly judge his character five years ago.

"I pray for mercy, my lord. A neighbor dropped off a little girl at my hut earlier. He said it was his niece, who was visiting, and he needed someone to watch her—"

"Leah?" Cristiana fell forward, knowing somehow this was her daughter.

The older woman clutched her garments as if to tear them, her face contorted with worry and fear.

"I did not know who it might be! I gave her to my eldest to watch while I went to hear the lord speak—"

"Take us to her." Duncan lifted the woman to her feet with one hand. "You are safe as long as you speak the truth."

"I do. I swear it." The woman stumbled forward, her feet moving fast now that she'd been set in motion. She wove around the burned cottages and hurried through the thick of the town where the huts were packed close together for warmth and protection. "I watch plenty of children often enough. Everyone knows I have an older girl who is good at it."

Cristiana's heart hammered so hard she could hardly hear the woman's words for the roaring of her blood through her veins. Duncan stepped in front of the older woman as she reached her hut. He pushed open the door.

Donegal of Culcanon stood in the archway.

They had been trapped.

Cristiana leaped back, clutching her sister. Edwina screamed. Duncan's half brother was much changed from the charming, handsome man Cristiana remembered from five summers ago. He bore some of Duncan's features, but the green-gold eyes that marked all of the Culcanons had turned darker, the skin around them lined with wrinkles from living outdoors these past moons, prey to the harsh Highland weather. His nose bore a crook that had not been there before, a testament to a lifetime of fighting. Even his expensive garb appeared tattered and careworn, a last vestige of wealth that he'd thrown away along with so much else.

Betrayal swam darkly before Cristiana's eyes, and she turned blindly on the woman who'd led them here. But instead of finding a target for her rage and fear, she saw her own emotions reflected in the older woman's gaze as the crofter's wife peered into the cottage.

Understanding came as she followed the villager's glance into the cottage behind Donegal.

In the darkness of the small shelter, Cristiana could see a huddle of children, big and small. They were a blur of dark cloaks and dirty gowns, work breeches and blankets as they clung together in a far corner.

A tall girl stood between Donegal and her smaller charges. A dog and a fat pig flanked her sides, as if to help fend off the filthy, treacherous outlaw brandishing a blade.

Perhaps the crofter's wife had no choice but to bring Cristiana with her—her own children put at risk as much as Leah.

"Mama!" A sweet, familiar voice piped up from under the pile of children, easing Cristiana's heart with relief so strong she might well have sank to the earth if not for Edwina holding her up. She could not yet see Leah, but she knew her voice.

"You dare threaten children now?" Duncan drew his blade with lightning speed, the sound of steel whipping through the air making a lethal hiss near her ears.

Cristiana guessed Donegal's only means of escape would be if he took a child with him. What could they do if he threatened Leah, or any of the little ones?

Donegal did not flinch.

"Why not?" he taunted. "I have nothing else to lose. I could not maintain a hold on Culcanon when people who were loyal to you refused to do my bidding any longer. I left with everything I could carry and all the people that I could convince to follow. But what does a man have if not land?"

Duncan shook his head, appearing as stunned at such a shortsighted vision as she felt.

"What of family? You had the support of your

father. Of me. You could have had a strong wife at your side—"

"And always be the second son?" Donegal scoffed as if that position meant less than nothing. "I was better off before your father recognized me. At least as a tradesmen's son, I was first in line to inherit a business, and all the women in my hometown were quick to barter favors for my skill. I was content until I found out I had been entitled to so much more growing up. As a bastard, I was less than nothing. A second son to a man who never would have recognized me if not for your self-righteous insistence."

"You weren't the only one who would have been better off," Edwina shouted from behind Cristiana.

Cristiana realized her sister was tense with fury. Outrage.

"You may have lost much, but at least your soul is still intact." Duncan pressed the sword closer to Donegal. "If you step near any of those children, you will lose that, too, along with your life."

An ugly twist of Donegal's features was their only warning. He rounded on the children, blade raised.

Cristiana's heart seized. The mother beside her screamed in unison with Edwina.

The dog within the cottage launched at the madman, but not as quickly as Duncan swung his blade. The blunt side of the sword connected with Donegal's ear, sending him to the floor in a slump.

Donegal's shout filled the hut, bringing the entire village into the street outside the cottage.

"It is finished," Duncan warned his half brother, lowering the point of his blade to the other man's chest while Donegal's temple bled onto the dirt floor.

Cristiana whispered prayers of thanksgiving, crossing herself as she vowed to repay Duncan for his unfailing sense of honor, that she had too often ignored.

"I came for my daughter." Donegal turned his head, to peer back at the cluster of children. His long, matted hair stuck to the ragged cloak that still bore the proud crest of the Culcanon clan.

A crest he did not deserve to wear.

"You have no family," Duncan told him, keeping his sword leveled at the thief's chest while Cullen worked his way into the cottage behind him.

From Cullen's dark glare, Cristiana guessed he would gladly sink his blade between the traitor's ribs and finish the matter here and now. But from what she knew of Duncan, she guessed that was not something he would allow. Donegal would face a punishment set by the king.

"Perhaps not," Donegal agreed, his eyes rolling back in his head before he refocused them, hatred still glinting along with the obvious pain. "I could not tell one dirty urchin from another."

And for that, Cristiana would remain forever grateful. She did not think Duncan's half brother would have escaped the town with Leah, not with everyone searching for them. Thanks to Duncan, Donegal had never gotten that far.

She rushed into the hut with Edwina and the older mother who lived at the cottage. The children swarmed them, needing to receive hugs as much as the women needed to give them. Tears clogged Cristiana's throat as she felt Leah's arms about her neck. Other small arms.

Behind them, the village streets overflowed with crofters and their families who came bearing simple weapons. Farm implements, blacksmiths' hammers and lots of clenched fists. Cristiana could hear the mother who'd led them to the cottage muttering a litany of prayers under her breath.

She'd been as much a victim as any of them, Cristiana felt certain.

For her part, Cristiana had faith that no further harm would come to any of the people of Culcanon. As a just and strong ruler, Duncan would protect them all.

"You have been called to your king to answer for your crimes," Duncan informed him, waving forward the village blacksmith's son, who carried forth a long, heavy chain with irons at each end. "Attacking Malcolm's envoys ranked as one of your most brainless acts, but it brings with it the promise of retribution. Until that time, you will answer your accusers here.

Lady Edwina, do you have anything to say to this man?"

Surprised that Duncan would allow Edwina to come face-to-face with her attacker, Cristiana turned to measure her sister's response.

Edwina's jaw tensed. She settled one of the young children onto the floor of the hut and marched up to the figure on the ground in a heap at her feet. Drawing herself up to her full height she pinned her shoulders back and spit in his face forcefully.

"You were never worthy to walk on the same earth as me." Edwina spun on her heel, but not before she kicked up a bit of dirt which landed on his face.

Cristiana noticed the filth clung to the place where she'd spit, but the craven pig did not dare to swipe at it with Duncan's sword at his chest.

"Anyone else?" Duncan called to the crowd while the blacksmith and his son put Donegal in irons and handed Duncan the key. "I will lock the outlaw in the dungeon for the night. Cullen of Blackstone will deliver the prisoner to our king in the morning."

At first, no one moved. And then a handful of young women seemed to find their courage. One by one, four brave females—crofters' daughters and young wives—followed Edwina's example. Each one spit in Donegal's eye, a spectacle that would have been amusing if it hadn't represented so much hurt.

Cristiana could see Duncan's surprise. His cold

fury. She wondered if his brother would live the night in captivity.

"Very well," Duncan said finally. "Cullen, he is yours to secure until morning."

It was a job Cullen seemed to relish. As the older knight shoved Donegal so hard he nearly fell to the ground, Cristiana could finally breathe easily, knowing Leah was forever out of Donegal's reach.

Wrapping her daughter in her arms, she wept her relief, all the more so to see that Leah had a circlet of woven willow branches about her wrist, a decoration someone must have made her while she was held captive these past hours.

Apparently, Edwina had already noted the bravery of the girl who had watched over Leah, for she had wrapped the young lady in a hug that made the crofter's daughter blush and giggle.

"You will be well rewarded," Cristiana assured the girl as she scooped up Leah and held her tight.

She did not know what role the mother had played in the treachery here, but she had faith Duncan would sort it out in due time.

Duncan stepped deeper into the dark hut behind them—she could tell by the way he eclipsed any sunlight in the cottage with his large frame. More than that, she had grown aware of his presence in a thousand little ways, her whole mind and body—and yes, her heart—uniquely attuned to him.

"The lass looks well, does she not?" Duncan's

voice was soft, but Cristiana heard the worry. The concern.

Her heart melted a little more for this man who had delivered her daughter safely back to her arms.

"I did not have my sword, Papa," Leah told him, her green eyes serious as she pouted prettily and tested a new name for Duncan. "But I was a very brave girl just the same. See what Aida made me?"

She held up the woven willow bracelet, far more interested in talking about her time with Aida than the man with the sword. Still, Cristiana would watch over her all the more carefully to be sure there were no lingering fears after the scare she'd suffered.

"Come." Duncan gestured toward the door of the hut. "I must put my lands to rights. But I will not be able to think about rebuilding until I know you are safe at home."

Cristiana followed Edwina out, adjusting Leah on her hip as she said goodbye to the children who'd been held hostage with Leah. Then, bracing herself against any tide of envy she'd once felt for the bond Edwina had with Leah, Cristiana handed the child over to her sister.

"I'll bet your aunt would like to carry you, too, sweeting," she told her little girl, kissing her forehead as she noted Edwina's surprise and gratitude. "She worried about you every bit as much as I did."

Edwina gave her a teary smile as she hugged the girl tight.

"It is true." She shifted the child in her arms as they walked alongside Cristiana. "I would have helped your mama chase that bad man all the way to London and back to make sure you were safe. But I knew the whole time your mother and father would rescue you."

In the language of sisters, Cristiana understood Edwina's simple assurance. She had not come home to take her child back to raise Leah as her own. She was comfortable with the decision she'd made long ago to give Leah to the woman who'd been ready to become a mother.

Cristiana's heart turned over in her chest.

Leah giggled and showed off her bracelet. Resilient. Strong. So much like her birth mother. Still, Cristiana's heart knew all the more ease to hear Edwina defer to Cristiana as Leah's mother.

Shifting her attention back to Duncan, Cristiana hurried to keep pace with him as he escorted them back to the squat keep that was his family's two-hundred-year-old seat.

"It will be good to breathe easier now that Donegal is captured and his minions are being sought," Cristiana noted, realizing suddenly how weak she was from the rush of so many emotions through her this day. "And perhaps I can start work on the inside of the keep now that I know we are safe from your half brother."

There was much to replace and repair. New

tapestries to weave or purchase. With her sister and daughter back at her side and Edwina's long hardship behind her, Cristiana looked forward to weddings. Edwina's. Her own.

"Nay." Duncan did not look her way, his demeanor cool and abrupt considering all they'd been through today. "When I said I want you safe at home, I did not mean here. I meant, you're going *home*. To Domhnaill."

"You cannot be serious."

Cristiana confronted him the moment he walked into his chamber late that night.

He'd told her hours ago that she would be going home and then he'd departed to help the villagers clean up the mess of the fire.

He hadn't really expected to see her here. Since they never had exchanged their vows and she had been uneasy about sharing a chamber anyway, he assumed she would take advantage of this time to visit with her sister or sit watch over Leah.

But even though he'd worked long past dark to clear the burned huts with his retainers and his tenants, Cristiana was wide awake when he stepped into the chamber.

"Whatever you're talking about, I'm sure I was very serious." He dropped his boots beside the door and laid his sword near the bed, wondering if she had any intention of sleeping here tonight. With him.

She'd been so angry with him about the way he'd taken Domhnaill that he wasn't sure what to expect from her anymore.

"Domhnaill." She followed him to the bed and began stripping off his cloak with surprising force. "You cannot wish to send me back there."

The topic interested him a great deal, even though he'd been trying to forget all day that he'd said such a thing.

Covering her busy hands with his, he slowed her efforts on the laces of his tunic, unsure why she wished to undress him.

Normally, he would not have minded. "I'm trying to be noble here, Cristiana. Would you leave the undressing to me?"

She frowned, her forehead crinkling in confusion.

"You will want to bathe. I already called for a tub when I heard your feet on the steps."

Male interest stirred, but he kept her hands prisoner while he spoke his peace.

"I will not keep you here when you believe yourself trapped into marriage." He had tried too hard to make things right between them to have this gulf of hurt always present. "I talked my way into your home, into marriage, into Domhnaill. And frankly, I will not give them up because your father cannot manage those lands. He not only endangers your people, he endangers all the Scots if he cannot secure the coast—"

"I know." Cristiana placed a hand on his lips. "I understand why you did it."

"But you do not appreciate my methods and you view it as a lack of trust."

"So you send me back to my father?" She scowled at him as she tossed his cape and the pin that had held it in place onto the floor. "Did I not have the right to be upset about that? But I might have understood if you'd explained it. At least, I like to think I would have. You never gave me that chance."

He did not move, thinking about her words as she lifted her fingers to his tunic laces again.

"At first, I could not afford to have you bar the gate to me and my men. Later, I came to care about you and—perhaps—I simply did not want to lose you." He took heart from the fact that she continued to undress him.

What if she was willing to forge ahead in spite of everything? Hope sparked faster than dry tinder.

"You complain that I think the worst of you, but how can I not think the worst when you will not tell me the truth?"

He understood. And while he did not necessarily like it, he had to believe she wanted to try again. Why else would she pull the linen of his tunic from the depths of his braies, sliding the fabric slowly across the places that called out for her touch?

Again, he had to halt her hands.

"The breaking of our betrothal cost me dearly. At

first, I told myself I only resented you because you robbed me of Domhnaill and a chance to unite our resources. I thought I could lose myself in war or with other women. But nothing eased the loss until I came back here to claim you. And I think that's because it was not the loss of Domhnaill I resented so much as the loss of you." It was the biggest truth he'd kept from her. The one thing she still did not know. "I have not told you because it seemed like too much power for a woman to have over me. But it is true, Cristiana. From that very first kiss by the wishing well all those years ago, you touched something within me. Something unlike anything else I had ever experienced."

She blinked, her eyes filling with what he hoped were happy tears.

"You truly do have a gift with words, Duncan the Brave." Her voice broke as a tear slipped free. "I love you dearly—then and now—even if I was too blinded by fears and uncertainty to be the woman you deserve. Also, the only way I could stay mad at you was to hold on to Edwina's hurt and make it my own. That's no excuse, though, for not fighting harder for you."

She shook her head helplessly. His heart lifted like a few thousand stone had been rolled off it. He'd been so determined to have her in his bed, as his wife, but he hadn't dared hope he would also win her heart in the process.

"It is in the past." Duncan kissed the tears on her

cheeks, hardly daring to believe he and Cristiana might have put the ugliness of long, dark years behind them. "Edwina is like a woman born anew around Cullen. Have you seen how she lights up?"

Cristiana smiled. "I understand the feeling well. Although if she marries him, who will I threaten to wed the next time I'm mad at you?"

He chuckled softly, so very grateful to have this clever, talented woman to bring joy and laughter to his days.

"That will not be a problem, since we will speak our vows in front of the priest the same day that Edwina and Cullen do. By the time Cullen returns from Malcolm's court, we will all ride to Domhnaill to meet him there and celebrate our good fortune with your father." He could not wait to make it official. "I admire how you took care of Domhnaill on your own even as the old laird's mind faded. You are a woman of rare talent and strength, and I want that by my side forever. I have loved you for as long as I've known you."

She wriggled her hands free of his and wrapped her arms about his neck.

"Truly?"

Her scent surrounded him, the sweet, welcoming fragrance of cloves and honey, clover and spring. He'd never forgotten it no matter how far he'd travelled from his homeland.

"Truly." He snaked his arms about her waist

and picked her up so that her body pressed fully against his.

"That is a very good thing. Although I have to confess that I will not reveal the location of your treasure until you marry me like a proper husband."

Surprise smacked him in the chest so hard he nearly dropped her.

"You've known where it was all this time?" He shook his head in disbelief and more than a little joy. "And you accuse me of keeping secrets?"

"No." She laughed and planted a kiss on his cheek. "The location came to me when I was a wreck about Leah. I was so scared and upset that I couldn't find my way to the children's chamber. And somehow, trying to force myself to remember the directions made me think about all the passages and stairwells at Domhnaill. When you think about it, the layouts of the keep are rather similar."

Puzzling through her words, he couldn't imagine how any of this had helped her find the treasure.

"I can see that." He picked her back up and brought her over to his bed, hoping the water bearers would not bring a tub anytime soon.

"I think that's why I got confused. The passages are so similar that I think the first lord of Culcanon designed his keep purposely like Domhnaill." She did not protest as he settled her across his lap, her skirts draping to the floor as he worked a slipper off her foot.

"Very likely." It amused him to think he'd been so concerned about finding that treasure once, but right now, the only riches he cared about were under his roof.

"Except some of the secret passages at Culcanon do not exist at Domhnaill. Yet that tangle of corridors around the children's chamber matches up well with the shape of your medallion—"

"By the rood, you are brilliant." He could see immediately what she meant, just by glancing down at the medallion on his chest. "He left the treasure in the keep in one of those old passages and then walled it up."

She grinned. "If we ride now, we could reach Domhnaill before the next nightfall. Edwina could watch over Leah for a few days. By this time tomorrow, we could hold dazzling riches in our hands."

"We already do," he reminded her. "And I have much better plans for this night."

He trailed his hand meaningfully up her leg.

"You do?" She settled against him more fully, her hip edging between his thighs.

"I love how distractible you are," he whispered in her ear, smoothing aside her hair to kiss the soft white column of her neck.

"Enough talking for one day," she chastised him, moving his hand to the ties up one side of her gown. "You need to show me your love."

Pulling her down to his chest, Duncan vowed to do his very best.

Epilogue

Four months later

"**P**apa, what about this one?" Leah held up a heavy necklace of gold and milky purple stones from the treasure they had discovered three days prior.

They all sat in the laird's solar at Domhnaill. Cristiana's father had cleared out his things and moved to a smaller chamber closer to the great hall. He swore it would be no trouble, even though Cristiana insisted they would not be in residence year-round. But sometimes he still came to the door, thinking his things were within his old chamber.

Today, her father was clear headed, however, and she savored every moment beside him. They had all gathered in Duncan's outer chamber to catalog the treasure unearthed at Domhnaill. Even Cullen and Edwina joined them.

"Those are amethysts," Duncan told Leah, dropping a kiss on the child's head as she tried on the necklace. "They might have come from Egypt, along with some of these coins."

He pointed to the heavy silver pieces with strange markings, part of a vast range of loot that had been walled up in Domhnaill's secret passages, unbeknownst to its in habitants for two hundred years.

"With what these are worth, you should be able to replace all those missing torch rings at Culcanon," Cullen remarked drily, his sense of humor sly and quiet and always sure to make his new wife laugh.

Edwina sat on his lap on the floor, where the two of them studied the coins. She had bloomed since she'd been back home. Her past seemed well behind her, although now and then she offered up some interesting bit of political intrigue from her days in King William's court. She was still reed-thin, but she had confided to Cristiana just that morning that she expected a child.

They had agreed to move into Culcanon for the half of the year that Duncan and Cristiana stayed at Domhnaill. For one thing, Edwina had been insistent that as Leah's "aunt," she wanted to see the child from time to time. And, inspired by Cristiana's advances in mead making, Edwina had taken quite an interest in the growing trade. She looked forward to working in the new mead house that Cristiana had convinced Duncan to build on Culcanon land.

"Perhaps." Duncan held up a hanging bowl inlaid with glass, white shell and elaborate filigree, a beautiful treasure in its own right. "Although with all the extravagant herbs my wife wishes to grow for her mead, I may need every cent of this to fund her brewing efforts."

Cristiana tugged his sleeve in smiling rebuke, knowing too well that Duncan was proud of her unique talent.

"Well, you cannot part with this piece," Edwina announced, holding up a gold-and-silver gilt chalice covered with rich etchings of maternal figures holding hands. The rounded bellies and full breasts of the characters marked the work as a pagan piece, but it held all the more significance to the Domhnaill sisters, since they were both expectant mothers.

"Do not show me," Cristiana teased, covering her own belly with her hand. "I cannot believe I will grow so round."

She was so thrilled to experience every moment of motherhood that she'd missed with Leah. Though she had watched Edwina's previous pregnancy, she had missed out on the joy of it as they had both been frightened over uncertain futures. Now, it seemed like divine providence that they could share the glad blessing of being new brides at the same time.

Although Cristiana was not only one moon along,

but over *four.* Duncan liked to tell her she must have conceived the moment he first touched her.

"Do not be foolish, my daughter," the old laird chastised, shaking a weathered finger in her direction. "Your mother was never more beautiful than when she expected our children."

His eyes misted a bit as if he was seeing his wife and not anyone else in the chamber. Cristiana and Edwina shared happy glances while Leah hopped off Duncan's lap and went over to her grandfather.

"This one should be your treasure," she told him, laying a heavy sword across his legs. "It has a boar on it for strength. Did you ever fight like a boar, Grandfather?"

While Cristiana's father launched into a tale from his warrior days, holding the sword aloft to act out the best parts, Duncan leaned close to Cristiana and whispered.

"You realize this is where she inherited her fierceness and her love of battle?" He pointed to the old laird and Leah curled on his lap, listening intently and following every twitch of the ancient blade with wide eyes.

Cristiana set aside his quill and ink and squeezed her hand between his, grateful for the moment of semi-privacy in the room full of family.

"Perhaps, but you hardly discourage her warrior ways with your toy swords and fighting lessons." She had debated calling Leah indoors on the warm spring mornings that Duncan had let the child play in the practice yard, but Leah seemed to be recovering so well from her scare with Donegal that she could not find it in her heart to dissuade the interest in swordplay.

"I must raise her to be as strong as her mother," Duncan whispered back, leaning close to kiss her cheek. "That is no easy task."

Her heart swelled with love as her eyes filled with tears. But then, she'd been quick to cry lately, her happiness surprising her at unexpected moments. She'd never been so happy. So loved.

"You are a wonderful father, Duncan the Brave." She cupped his face in her hand, falling under the spell of his deep green gaze.

"And you are a wife worth waiting five years for, Cristiana." He returned her kiss, his mouth awakening a fire inside her despite all the people around them. "Having you is every bit as sweet as I imagined."

Tilting her head to his, she reveled in one of life's perfect moments.

* * * * *

COMING NEXT MONTH FROM

HARLEQUIN®
HISTORICAL

Available January 25, 2011.

- **LADY LAVENDER**
  by **Lynna Banning**
  (Western)

- **SOCIETY'S MOST DISREPUTABLE GENTLEMAN**
  by **Julia Justiss**
  (Regency)

- **MARRIED: THE VIRGIN WIDOW**
  by **Deborah Hale**
  (Regency)
  Gentlemen of Fortune

- **A THOROUGHLY COMPROMISED LADY**
  by **Bronwyn Scott**
  (Regency)

REQUEST YOUR FREE BOOKS!

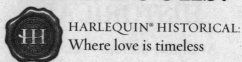

HARLEQUIN® HISTORICAL:
Where love is timeless

2 FREE NOVELS PLUS 2 **FREE GIFTS!**

YES! Please send me 2 FREE Harlequin® Historical novels and my 2 FREE gifts (gifts are worth about $10). After receiving them, if I don't wish to receive any more books, I can return the shipping statement marked "cancel." If I don't cancel, I will receive 6 brand-new novels every month and be billed just $4.94 per book in the U.S. or $5.49 per book in Canada. That's a saving of 20% off the cover price! It's quite a bargain! Shipping and handling is just 50¢ per book.* I understand that accepting the 2 free books and gifts places me under no obligation to buy anything. I can always return a shipment and cancel at any time. Even if I never buy another book from Harlequin, the two free books and gifts are mine to keep forever.

246/349 HDN E5L4

Name _____ (PLEASE PRINT) _____

Address _____ Apt. # _____

City _____ State/Prov. _____ Zip/Postal Code _____

Signature (if under 18, a parent or guardian must sign) _____

Mail to the **Harlequin Reader Service:**
IN U.S.A.: P.O. Box 1867, Buffalo, NY 14240-1867
IN CANADA: P.O. Box 609, Fort Erie, Ontario L2A 5X3

Not valid for current subscribers to Harlequin Historical books.

Want to try two free books from another line?
Call 1-800-873-8635 or visit www.morefreebooks.com.

* Terms and prices subject to change without notice. Prices do not include applicable taxes. N.Y. residents add applicable sales tax. Canadian residents will be charged applicable provincial taxes and GST. Offer not valid in Quebec. This offer is limited to one order per household. All orders subject to approval. Credit or debit balances in a customer's account(s) may be offset by any other outstanding balance owed by or to the customer. Please allow 4 to 6 weeks for delivery. Offer available while quantities last.

Your Privacy: Harlequin Books is committed to protecting your privacy. Our Privacy Policy is available online at www.eHarlequin.com or upon request from the Reader Service. From time to time we make our lists of customers available to reputable third parties who may have a product or service of interest to you. If you would prefer we not share your name and address, please check here. ☐

Help us get it right—We strive for accurate, respectful and relevant communications. To clarify or modify your communication preferences, visit us at www.ReaderService.com/consumerchoice.

HH10R

*Harlequin Romance author Donna Alward is loved
for her gorgeous rancher heroes.*

*Meet Wyatt as he's confronted by both a precious
little pink bundle left on his doorstep and his neighbor Elli
who's going to show him the ropes....*

Introducing
PROUD RANCHER, PRECIOUS BUNDLE

THE SQUAWKING QUIETED as Elli picked the baby up, and
Wyatt turned around, trying hard to ignore the feelings of
inadequacy as Darcy immediately stopped fussing.

"Maybe she's uncomfortable. What do you think, sweet-
heart?" Elli turned her conversation to the baby.

"What do you think is wrong?" Wyatt asked, putting the
coffee pot back on the burner.

A strange look passed over Elli's face, one that looked
like guilt and panic. But it was gone quickly. "I couldn't
say," she replied.

"But you were so good with her this afternoon." Wyatt
put his hands on his hips.

"Lucky, that's all. I just...remembered a few things."
The same strange look flitted over her features once more.

Wyatt took the coffee to the table. "You fooled me. You
looked like you knew exactly what you were doing." So
much so that Wyatt had felt completely inept. A feeling he
despised. He was used to being the one in control.

Elli and Darcy walked the length of the kitchen and
back. After a few moments, she admitted, "I haven't really
cared for a baby before. The things I thought of were simply
things I'd heard about. Not from experience, Mr. Black."

Her chin jutted up, closing the subject but making him

want to ask the questions now pulsing through his mind. But then he remembered the old saying—*Don't look a gift horse in the mouth.* He'd benefit from whatever insight she had and be glad of it.

"I don't really know what babies need," he said. "I fed her, patted her back like you did, walked her to sleep, but every time I put her down…"

Wyatt almost groaned. Of course. He'd forgotten one important thing. He'd been so focused on getting the formula the right temperature that he'd forgotten to check her diaper. Not that he had any clue what to do there either.

Pulling calves and shoveling out stalls was far less intimidating than one tiny newborn.

"She's probably due for a diaper change, isn't she." He tried to sound nonchalant. This was a perfect opportunity. Elli must know how to change a diaper. He could simply watch her so he'd know better for the next time.

Instead, Elli came around the corner of the counter and placed Darcy back in his arms. "Here you go, Uncle Wyatt," she said lightly. "You get diaper duty. I'll fix the coffee. Cream and sugar?"

Oh boy, Wyatt thought, looking down into Darcy's pursed face, his smug plan blown to smithereens. He was in for it now.

Will sparks fly between Elli and Wyatt?

Find out in
PROUD RANCHER, PRECIOUS BUNDLE
Available February 2011 from Harlequin Romance

Try these Healthy and Delicious Spring Rolls!

INGREDIENTS

2 packages rice-paper
spring roll wrappers
(20 wrappers)

1 cup grated carrot

¼ cup bean sprouts

1 cucumber, julienned

1 red bell pepper, without
stem and seeds, julienned

4 green onions
finely chopped—
use only the green part

DIRECTIONS

1. Soak one rice-paper wrapper
   in a large bowl of hot water
   until softened.

2. Place a pinch each of carrots,
   sprouts, cucumber, bell
   pepper and green onion on the
   wrapper toward the bottom
   third of the rice paper.

3. Fold ends in and roll tightly
   to enclose filling.

4. Repeat with remaining
   wrappers. Chill before
   serving.

Find this and many more delectable recipes
including the perfect dipping sauce in